D1274757

Gabriel's
Clock

Gabriel's Clock

by
Hilton Pashley

HOUGHTON MIFFLIN HARCOURT
Boston New York

www.hmhco.com

The text of this book is set in Horley Old Style MT.
The illustrations are rendered in mixed media.
Illustration © 2014 by August Hall.

Library of Congress Cataloging-in-Publication Data
Pashley, Hilton.
Gabriel's clock / by Hilton Pashley.
p. cm.
Originally published by Andersen Press in 2013.
Summary: "Twelve-year-old Jonathan is half-angel, half-demon, and the only one of his kind. But he has no idea of his true identity, and now a rogue archdemon wants him for his own sinister purpose." — Provided by publisher
ISBN 978-0-544-30176-4
[1. Angels—Fiction. 2. Demonology—Fiction. 3. Good and evil—Fiction.
4. Identity—Fiction.] I. Title.
PZ7.P26915Gab 2014
[Fic]—dc23
2013042012

Manufactured in the United States
DOC 10 9 8 7 6 5 4 3 2 1
4500491770

for the real angela and jonathan

Contents

Gabriel's
Clock

Chapter 1
JONATHAN

In the blink of an eye Jonathan's life changed forever. Not moments before, he'd been sitting in the cottage kitchen eating his dinner; now he was hurtling down the cellar steps as three black shapes burst through the living room window.

Jonathan's mother screamed and pulled him across the cluttered cellar while his father slammed the door shut behind them. With a shaking hand he turned a rusty iron key in the lock and backed away, his face pale.

"What's happening?" cried Jonathan. "Who is that? Why are they breaking into our house?"

His father looked at him and shook his head wordlessly. For the first time in his life Jonathan realized what true fear looked like—stark, naked, gut-churning fear. He watched in terror as the cellar door rattled on its hinges. The room shook with the force of the blows, dust sifting from the ceiling like icing sugar.

"They've found us!" said his father.

"Who've found us?" Jonathan cried. "I don't understand!"

His mother held him tightly, kissing the crown of his head, squeezing her eyes shut to keep tears from falling into his hair. "I'm sorry, Jonathan," she whispered to him. "I'm so sorry; we tried so hard to protect you!"

With an awful crack a huge fist punched its way through the door, splintering the ancient wood like kindling. The fist withdrew, and through the gap a face peered in at the huddled family. The face had no visible features, just a smooth expanse of skin between hairline and shirt collar.

Jonathan screamed and pointed as the face smiled— if the sudden appearance of a crimson slit filled with jagged teeth could be called a smile.

"It's Crow," gasped Jonathan's father. He turned to his wife and whispered in her ear. "You know where to take our boy. Use the old coal chute in the corner; it's the only way out. I'll hold them off for as long as I can." He kissed her cheek and hugged his son. "Be brave," he said, looking straight into Jonathan's extraordinarily blue eyes. "Now go!"

"We're not just leaving you, Dad."

"*I said, go!*" Jonathan's father roared.

An awful, gurgling laugh erupted from outside the room. With one last massive blow, the door was torn from its hinges and reduced to matchwood. Into the room stepped three humanoid figures, each wearing shiny black shoes, an immaculately tailored pinstriped suit, and a bowler hat.

The first, Crow, was a hulking brute; his apelike arms dangled so low, his knuckles almost brushed the floor. Another was short and thin, with long dark hair falling to her waist. The last figure stood between the other two; tall and menacing, he spread his arms wide to reveal overlong fingers tipped with cruel talons. None of the three had anything resembling a face—just those terrible smiles.

Jonathan's mother grabbed his hand and half dragged him to an open bunker in the far corner of the cellar. Behind them, slick with black dust, a disused coal chute led up to an old wooden hatch. Beyond it lay the last rays of sunset, and escape.

The tallest figure stepped forward, his attention fixed on Jonathan. "*Boy!*" he hissed, triumph dripping from the word like rancid fat.

Jonathan froze, his mind shrieking at him that this wasn't happening. This sort of thing only happened in nightmares. It wasn't *real*.

From the corner, he watched as his father grabbed a short length of scaffolding pole that lay propped against the cellar wall. Jonathan fully expected him to launch himself at the monsters that had invaded their home. Instead, and with extraordinary strength, his father swung at the huge brick pillar in the middle of the cellar floor, tearing through it like paper.

"Missed me," said the tall monster.

Jonathan's father smiled grimly and shook his head, then Jonathan felt himself pulled off his feet and onto a pile of cobwebbed coal as the old cottage let out a groan of pain. He stared as the ceiling, and a great deal of the cottage, collapsed into the cellar. It was as if a giant hand made of masonry and wood had just slammed down onto his father and the three monsters, wiping them from view.

Dust and sound exploded all around him, and Jonathan fought his mother as she tried to pull him away.

"*Dad!*" he screamed. "*Dad!*"

Suddenly his fear left him, and it was replaced by something else entirely, an emotion with which he was completely unfamiliar: cold fury. Jonathan gasped as the muscles in his shoulders and back began to howl in pain. It was like something that was buried under his skin was trying to tear itself free.

"Jonathan!" his mother begged as she dragged him bodily into the filthy coal chute. "We have to go; the whole cottage is about to—"

With a crack like a pistol shot, a wooden beam sheared from the wall above and swung down, striking Jonathan behind his right ear. He slumped in his mother's arms, his vision narrowed to a small, dim tunnel. A wet sensation ran down his neck, and he absently raised shaking fingers to the back of his head. He felt bone move, and a flare of agony lit up the inside of his skull like a firework.

His limbs virtually useless, Jonathan felt himself dragged upward and out into the fresh air, away from the choking brick dust and the noise of his collapsing home. He lay on damp grass, staring at the huge orange ball of the setting sun, looking at the patterns it made as it lanced through the clouds. He tried reaching out to touch it, but his arms wouldn't move.

There was a noise of a car engine being started, and Jonathan was half carried, half dragged, toward it. The world tilted as he was gently laid on something soft, his legs drawn up to his chest. He thought he could hear something. It sounded like his mother weeping uncontrollably, and he moved his lips to tell her not to be sad, but no sound came out, just a small bubble of blood.

He rocked gently on the seat of the car as his mother drove away from the cottage as fast as she could, not daring to look back in case she saw a faceless figure in a suit and bowler hat running down the road behind her.

"Where . . . we . . . going?" Jonathan managed to mumble.

"I'm taking you home, darling," said his mother, her voice thick with an emotion he didn't recognize. "I'm taking you home. Just hold on. Please just hold on."

"S'okay . . . Mom. I'll . . . hold . . . on."

A choked sob was her only reply. Jonathan watched the flickering light of sunset through the car windows above him. He watched as it dimmed, then failed completely, leaving him in darkness. The roar of the engine and the hum of the tires on the road cradled him as he tried not to fall asleep. He didn't know why, but he feared that if he fell asleep now, he might not wake up.

After what seemed like an age, the sound of asphalt was replaced by the soft crunch of leaves and small branches. The car drew to a gentle halt, and Jonathan felt himself lifted from the back seat, his mother's arm supporting him with extraordinary strength. The warm air of a summer night brushed his face as he stumbled along, his feet stubbornly refusing to put themselves one in front of the other. The throbbing at the back of his head was rapidly becoming his entire world.

Leaves and wood gave way to grass, and Jonathan felt something tingling at the edge of his consciousness, something that dulled the ache in his skull. It was like someone was holding a cold washcloth to his forehead while whispering words of comfort in his ear. He smiled to himself, then gave in to the need to drift away.

Jonathan's mother sensed the change in her son, and with the last of her strength she dragged his leaden body the few remaining steps to her destination—a little cottage tucked away in a graveyard behind a church. Sinking to her knees with Jonathan in her lap, she pounded her fist against the door.

"Please," she sobbed under her breath. "Please, Gabriel."

There came a muffled thumping from inside the cottage. "All right, I'm coming," said a sleep-sodden voice.

The door was yanked open, and an old man in bare feet and a linen nightshirt peered out. He stared open-mouthed when he saw who was sprawled on his doorstep. Jonathan's mother looked up at him, the imperial purple of her almond-shaped eyes almost black in the half-light while her tattered robes revealed a tracery of crimson scales that patterned her neck from behind her pointed ears right down to her shoulders. Delicate horns grew from her forehead and curved over her skull, almost meeting the batlike wings that lay limp across her back.

"Savantha?" gasped Gabriel. "Jonathan?" The old angel sagged against the door frame and shut his eyes. "Belial came for you, didn't he? I told you to stay here with me, where you'd be safe." He shook his head in despair.

"Please help me," begged Savantha, holding out a hand. "I'm so tired. I can't maintain Jonathan's disguise as well as my own."

Gabriel embraced them. "Come inside," he said. "Before anyone sees you." Leaning down, he half carried his visitors into the cottage.

"He's badly hurt," said Savantha, tears running down her face as she laid Jonathan on the sofa. "Darriel destroyed the cottage to bury the Corvidae, and a beam hit Jonathan's head. I don't know how to stop the bleeding . . ."

Gabriel kneeled beside them and gently slipped his hand beneath Jonathan's blood-matted hair. He briefly closed his eyes in concentration; his will focused on the boy's injuries.

"His skull's fractured, and he's lost a lot of blood." Savantha let out a small cry.

"I can fix it," said Gabriel, squeezing her hand in reassurance. He paused, shut his eyes again, and took a deep breath. The air around Jonathan's head shimmered and brightened, filled with ever-shifting mathematical symbols. A smell of apples and beeswax filled the room, and Savantha watched in awe as her father-in-law performed a miracle as simply as if he were drawing the curtains.

Jonathan let out a sigh, and his breathing became regular and deep. Color returned to his cheeks, and Savantha shook with a mixture of relief and exhaustion.

"Thank you, Gabriel," she whispered.

Gabriel nodded, his lips set in a thin line. "Where is Darriel, Savantha? Where is my son?"

"We'd run to the cellar," she said. "Darriel knocked out the floor supports and dropped the cottage on Rook, Raven, and Crow so we could escape." She began to cry again. "He was buried with them. I don't know what's happened to him. Maybe he managed to get away and he's following us."

"Maybe," said Gabriel. "But the demons of the Corvidae are strong, Savantha—that's why Belial uses them. Darriel is a match for one of them, but all three at once?" The angel shook his head. "This is exactly why I wanted you to live here in Hobbes End with me, not try to face the world alone."

"But Darriel—"

"My son is as stubborn as his father," said Gabriel. "And proud, too, which is a common fault with us angels."

"I've got to go see if Darriel's still alive!"

"I know," said Gabriel. "But you're exhausted; you need to catch your breath first. I'll get you something to drink."

Savantha nodded, and Gabriel swiftly returned with a steaming mug of tea. As he handed it to her, his face turned ashen and he let out a racking cough.

"What's wrong?" asked Savantha.

"You know what's wrong," said Gabriel, perching on the arm of the sofa. "I don't have much power left. Every time I use some, I'm left weaker than before. That's the price I pay for losing my wings."

"I'm sorry," said Savantha.

"Don't be," replied Gabriel. "It was my choice to give them away to create this village, to give my beloved Hobbes End a soul. I wouldn't take my power back even if I could—it would be murder. Anyway, what kind of grandfather would I be if I didn't help my grandson when he needed me?"

Savantha smiled. "You're an angel."

"Ha-de-ha." Gabriel smiled back. Then, looking down at Jonathan with a mixture of wonder and sadness, he reached out and brushed a stray lock of hair from his grandson's face. "The power inside him is very strong now. I can feel it—all that potential just waiting for him to learn how to access it. It was obvious when he was born, and now it's shining out like a beacon. It's no wonder Belial managed to find you."

Savantha put her head in her hands. "We stayed in one place too long. We hadn't seen any sign of Belial and the Corvidae for such a long time. We thought we were safe . . ."

Gabriel sighed. "Jonathan will never be safe, Savantha. Not until he's old enough and strong enough to face an archdemon by himself. Until then, Belial will keep trying to catch him. Jonathan's the only half-angel, half-demon child in existence, and for some reason he's been blessed with more raw power than I believed possible. I see him as someone both Heaven and Hell could rally behind; but Belial, he just sees him as a potential weapon—a means to carry on a grudge that should have been forgotten centuries ago." Gabriel angrily thumped his fist against the sofa.

Savantha reached out and squeezed the old angel's hand. "Will you look after Jonathan for me while I go find my husband? Will you keep my boy safe?"

"You don't have to ask," said Gabriel. "Although I think it's best if his true appearance stays hidden for the moment. I'd trust the inhabitants of this village with my life, but there's no point broadcasting Jonathan's presence. I take it my grandson still knows nothing of what he is?"

Savantha shook her head. "We've kept everything hidden from him, tried to let him lead a normal life." She smiled ruefully. "He thinks his parents are called Daniel and Sarah, and that his dad works in some top-secret government department. Imagine if he suddenly looked in the mirror one morning and saw *this*."

She moved her hand slowly over Jonathan's face, the air shimmering as she did so. His features remained the same but with two startling additions: a budding pair of horns protruded from his temples, and a tracery of crimson scales similar to his mother's peeped out from the neck of his sweatshirt.

With another wave of Savantha's hand, Jonathan's horns and crimson scales disappeared. "The masking should hold until he learns how to do it himself," she said. "Let's maintain the lie as long as we can, keep him safe."

"He doesn't know who I am, does he?" asked Gabriel.

Savantha shook her head sadly.

"Well, it's probably for the best," said Gabriel. "If we're going to hide Jonathan from Belial and the Corvidae, then we need to keep him away from me for his own safety. The best person to look after him is Igna-tius. He'd love to have a child running around the vicar-age again."

Savantha took her sleeping son's hand. "And while you look after Jonathan, I can find Darriel."

"What if you can't?" asked Gabriel.

"Then I'm going to petition Lucifer for help. It's time he stopped sitting on the fence and did something about rogue archdemons."

Gabriel raised his eyebrows in surprise. "That's brave."

Savantha snorted. "Lucifer doesn't scare me. If Heaven won't do anything about Belial, then maybe Hell should."

"I can't argue with that," said Gabriel. "But, please, be as quick as you can. Jonathan will be out cold for a few days, but when he wakes up in a strange place, with-out you or his father, surrounded by people he's never met, he's going to be scared and will ask a lot of awkward questions."

"I know," said Savantha. "I don't want to be away from him a moment longer than I have to. But until I get back, you'll need to . . ."

"Lie to him?"

She nodded.

"So be it," said Gabriel.

Savantha turned to look at Jonathan. "I can't even say goodbye."

Gabriel shook his head. "We'll keep Jonathan safe. Now go and bring my son back to me."

Her face wretched, Savantha bent over Jonathan, kissed him gently on the cheek, and whispered farewell.

Chapter 2
I'm Too Old for This

Gabriel sat and looked at Jonathan as he slept on the sofa.

"You'll be safe here in Hobbes End, Jonathan," said Gabriel. "I won't let Belial hurt you."

He sighed and got to his feet. Grabbing an overcoat from a hook by the door and slipping on a pair of shoes, he quietly left his cottage, locking the door behind him. He made his way through the churchyard and along the road to the vicarage. He smiled when he saw a light on in one of the ground-floor rooms. "Oh, Ignatius. Burning the midnight oil again, are we?"

The vicarage was surrounded by a high stone wall, with a pair of huge, wrought-iron gates leading onto a gravel drive. They were always open, and on each of the gateposts sat a granite gargoyle. Their eyes were closed, and they were snoring. Not wanting to explain why he was creeping into the vicarage in the middle of the night, Gabriel tried to tiptoe past but was foiled by the crunch of his shoes on gravel.

"Who goes there?" the gargoyles said in unison.

"Montgomery, Stubbs," said Gabriel, "I need to see Ignatius; sorry to wake you up when you're on guard duty."

"That's okay, Gabriel," chorused the gargoyles. "Why are you wearing your nightshirt under your coat?"

The angel grinned. "Look, we've had a new arrival in the village. I can't explain yet, but I need both of you to keep quiet about anything you see tonight. Will you do that for me?"

"You can trust us," they said. "Cross our hearts and hope to die."

"Hopefully it won't come to that, but I suggest you pretend to be fast asleep until the sun comes up, okay?"

The gargoyles nodded, shut their eyes, and began snoring again, very unconvincingly. Shaking his head, Gabriel continued up the drive until he reached the front door. Rather than use the brass bell pull, he gave a gentle knock. There was a pause, then footsteps, and the door opened to reveal a massive shape that almost blotted out the light from the hallway.

"Gabriel?" boomed a deep baritone voice.

"Good evening, Grimm. My apologies for the lateness of my visit, but I need to see Ignatius."

"That sounds serious — you'd better come in."

Gabriel stepped into the vicarage and followed Grimm down the hall to the kitchen.

"Take a seat and I'll put the kettle on. Ignatius will be through in a bit; he's just writing in his journal."

Gabriel smiled and nodded, watching Grimm as he went about one of his favorite activities: making tea. Halcyon Grimm was possibly the biggest human being Gabriel had ever known. He was less a man and more a piece of artillery. With his bald head, caterpillar eyebrows, and badly broken nose, Grimm wouldn't have looked out of place as a circus strongman. Luckily for everyone he came into contact with, though, his quick smile and gentleness soon put people at ease.

"Hello, Gabriel. To what do we owe such an unexpected visit?" The angel turned to see Ignatius Crumb, vicar of Hobbes End, standing in the kitchen doorway with an unlit pipe tucked into the corner of his mouth — he had given up smoking years earlier but still liked the feel of his old pipe in his mouth.

"We have a problem," said Gabriel. "I need you both to come with me to my cottage."

"What's wrong?" asked Ignatius.

Gabriel had just opened his mouth to speak when the flap in the back door banged open and a large black cat with white front paws and a dead bird in his mouth jumped into the room. The cat looked up, realized that all three men were looking at him, and froze. His jaw opened with theatrical slowness, and the soggy-feathered corpse fell to the floor. The silence was deafening.

"What?" said the cat. "Why is everyone staring at me? Stop it. You're freaking me out!"

"You're not going to leave that there are you, Elgar?" said Grimm.

"Well, I was intending to nibble on it later, but now I've lost my appetite."

"Then clear it away," growled Grimm.

"Fine," huffed the cat, picking up the bird with his teeth and dropping it in the bin. He jumped onto the kitchen table and started washing his ears. "Nice jimjams, Gabriel. What brings *you* out for a midnight stroll?"

The angel put his head in his hands and sighed. "I am too old for this."

Ten minutes later, Ignatius and Grimm were standing in Gabriel's cottage, staring at the wounded boy lying on the sofa.

"Who is he?" asked Ignatius.

"He's my grandson," said Gabriel.

Ignatius's pipe fell out of his mouth and landed on the carpet. "I didn't know you had a grandson!"

"It's complicated," said Gabriel. "This is Jonathan, and he's in a great deal of trouble."

"What kind of trouble?" asked Grimm.

"The kind that involves being hunted by an archdemon. And tonight Belial found him. I've been dreading this ever since Jonathan was born."

"Belial!" gasped Ignatius. "What on earth would he want with your grandson?"

Gabriel sighed. "I know Jonathan looks like an ordinary boy, but he isn't. His father is my son, Darriel . . . but his mother, Savantha, is a demon from the area of Hell controlled by Belial."

"You mean . . . ?" stammered Ignatius.

Gabriel nodded. "Yes. My grandson is the only half-angel, half-demon child in all of creation."

"But I thought that was impossible," said Grimm.

"It is," said Gabriel. "Or rather, it was supposed to be. Apparently creation has other ideas. Perhaps times are changing for Heaven and Hell as we know it?"

Ignatius picked up his pipe and ran his fingers through his hair. "Well, I didn't see that coming. Why didn't you tell us about this before?"

"I'm sorry," said Gabriel. "I didn't want to burden

you. Not that I had much say in the matter, since my son is even more stubborn than I am. I wanted Jonathan and his parents to stay here in Hobbes End, where they would have been safe, but Darriel wanted to do it all himself, try to let Jonathan have a 'normal' life — as if that was ever going to happen." He shook his head sadly. "As soon as word of Jonathan's existence started to spread, it was only a matter of time before one of the three archdemons — Belial, Baal, or Lilith — disobeyed Lucifer and made a grab for power."

"But what does Belial want with Jonathan?" asked Ignatius.

"Jonathan is special," said Gabriel. "I can sense it in him, and so can Belial. Because of the mixed bloodlines of the demonic and the divine, Jonathan has the potential to become something quite extraordinary. Greater than me or my siblings, greater even than Lucifer himself. Belial will want to twist him, control him, use him. Turn my grandson into a weapon. I will not let that happen."

"I see." Ignatius nodded, his face grave.

"And not only do we have Belial to contend with, he's brought his bogeymen with him too. He's unleashed the Corvidae."

"I thought they were just a myth," said Grimm. He

turned to Ignatius. "I remember your dad telling us scary stories about them when we were kids."

"Oh, they're real," said Ignatius. "They've been popping up for the best part of a century, and wherever they go they leave nothing but destruction in their wake. They currently have an appetite for wearing human skin, pinstriped suits, and bowler hats in order to hide their true forms."

"I don't like the sound of that," said Grimm. "I may have to hit them with my cricket bat."

"Hopefully you won't get the chance," said Gabriel. "As you know, Hobbes End will not allow anything evil to cross its borders and live. I designed it that way. Jonathan will be safe — as long as he doesn't leave here."

"So, how did he end up on your sofa with a nasty head wound?" asked Grimm, kneeling to examine the boy's injuries.

"The Corvidae finally caught up with him," sighed Gabriel. "Ever since he was born, Jonathan's parents have been running, moving from place to place, not settling anywhere. They wanted to be a normal family so badly that this time they stayed in one place just that little bit too long. Darriel held off the Corvidae long enough for Savantha to escape and bring Jonathan here, but as you can see, Jonathan got hurt in the process."

"Well, you did a good job stopping the bleeding," said Grimm, gently probing Jonathan's scalp. "And his skull feels intact, but there's still lots of swelling. He'll need a week or so of bed rest before he's fit enough to be up and about."

"Anyone would think you knew something about cuts and bruises." Ignatius smiled, teasing his friend a little.

"Halcyon Nathaniel Oberon Grimm, M.D., if you please," said Grimm. "I think a medical degree and years of experience as an army doctor have taught me something about anatomy."

"Where are Savantha and Darriel now?" asked Ignatius.

Gabriel looked unbearably sad. "I don't know," he said. "Savantha left Jonathan with me and went straight back to find Darriel. To see if . . ."

"He's dead?" asked Ignatius.

"Or worse," said Gabriel. "My son is strong, but he's no match for monsters like the Corvidae — not all three of them. If they take him alive, then Belial will have him." Gabriel shuddered as a single tear ran down his cheek. "And if Belial has Darriel, then my son might, under duress, give away Jonathan's location. Belial will suspect that Savantha may bring Jonathan here, but he'll want to make sure of where his prey is running to before he makes his move."

Ignatius placed a reassuring hand on Gabriel's shoulder. "Don't despair yet, old friend."

"I'll try not to," said Gabriel. "But it feels like everything is unraveling and there's nothing I can do to stop it."

"Will Savantha come back here if she can't find Darriel?" asked Grimm.

Gabriel shook his head. "No, she's even more headstrong than my son. If she can't find Darriel, then she'll go and petition Lucifer for aid."

Ignatius puffed out his cheeks and exhaled. "I see. Well, what would you like us to do in the meantime?"

"I need you to look after Jonathan, keep him safe until his parents come back. If he lives here with me, it may draw unwanted attention. You can pretend that he's simply a new arrival in the village who's been hurt and needs to be cared for."

"And will Jonathan agree to this?" asked Ignatius. "Won't he want to stay with his grandfather?"

Gabriel sighed. "Jonathan doesn't know what he is. He thinks his name is Jonathan Smith and that he's had to move house a lot because his father works for the government on matters of national security. He even thinks his parents' names are Daniel and Sarah."

"'Oh, what a tangled web we weave,'" said Ignatius, shaking his head.

"Jonathan has never heard of Hobbes End, and he doesn't know I exist. He was six days old the last time I saw him. Hobbes End knows *him*, however. Jonathan is the only child to have been born in the village since Grimm."

"He was born here?" spluttered Ignatius. "Why didn't you say something? Why didn't you trust me with this?"

Gabriel just looked sad.

"I get it," said Ignatius with a rueful smile. "Angels are stubborn."

Gabriel nodded. "Jonathan was born right here in this cottage twelve years ago. I begged Darriel and Savantha to stay, but they just wouldn't listen. Families, sometimes they break your heart." He wiped his eyes on the sleeve of his coat. "Will you help me?" he asked. "Will you help him?"

"You know we will," rumbled Grimm, gently picking up Jonathan and cradling him in his huge arms.

"Hobbes End will always look after those who need somewhere to be safe," said Ignatius, reaching out and squeezing the still-sleeping Jonathan's hand. "Come on, Grimm, it's time we took him home."

Grimm nodded and turned to go.

"We'll talk more tomorrow," said Gabriel. "Things will work out. You'll see."

Leaving the angel alone in his cottage, Grimm and Ignatius walked slowly back to the vicarage.

"Are you going to be all right with this?" asked Grimm.

"I'm not comfortable with lying to Jonathan about his heritage once he wakes up, but we don't have much choice if we're going to protect him."

"I wasn't talking about that," said Grimm. "I was thinking that you haven't had a kid living in the house since . . ."

"Since the accident?" said Ignatius, his voice unintentionally sharp.

"Yeah," said Grimm as they marched along in the moonlight. "Since the accident."

"Sorry," said Ignatius. "Whenever I think about Angela and David, I get all defensive. It's been three years, and I'm still mourning them."

"I miss them too, you know," said Grimm. "Angela was always a good friend to me, and little David was my godson, bless him. Look, Ignatius, we've been mates since we were kids, and I'm telling you that you need to let your grief over your wife and son go. I can mend most injuries, but I can't mend a broken heart."

"I know," said Ignatius. "I just wish that I could say goodbye to them and know that they heard me." He sighed heavily.

"Well," said Grimm, "we're going to have our hands full for the foreseeable future, so maybe that'll stop you getting all maudlin."

Ignatius grinned. "Is Oberon really one of your middle names? You never told me that before."

"It's true," said Grimm. "But if you tell Elgar, I will thump you, vicar or not."

"Then your secret is safe with me."

Not needing to say anything else, the two old friends walked home in silence.

From her bedroom window on the other side of the village green, a wide-awake Cay Forrester stared in astonishment as Ignatius and Grimm carried what looked like a sleeping boy from the churchyard to the vicarage.

"Oh, this is just brilliant," she said to herself. "Tomorrow could quite possibly be the most exciting day of my entire life!"

Chapter 3

CAY AND CONSPIRACY

The sun barely had time to burn the mist off the village pond before Cay had streaked out of her house, run across the green, and skidded to a halt at the vicarage gates. From their perches, two granite gargoyles peered down at her.

"Guys, guys, you'll never guess what."

"What?" asked Stubbs. He turned to his friend. "What does she want, Mr. Montgomery?"

"I think she wants us to ask her why she's all excited."

Cay nodded.

"Over to you, Mr. Stubbs," said Montgomery with a grin.

"Oh, goody," said Stubbs, rubbing his paws together. "Why are you all excited, Cay?"

"Because I've finally got someone to hang out with! I've been the only kid in the village, like, forever, and I saw Grimm and Ignatius carrying a boy over here last night. Is he awake? Can I see him? Can I?"

Stubbs looked at Montgomery in panic. "What boy?" he said, sounding very unsure of himself.

"The one they brought here last night. I saw them!"

"I didn't see anyone carry an unconscious boy into the vicarage last night," said Stubbs, watching uncomprehendingly as Montgomery repeatedly drew his hand across his mouth in a zipping motion.

"Aha!" cried Cay, her auburn ponytail swinging wildly as she jumped up and down on the spot. "Gotcha. You did see them."

Montgomery clapped his hand to his forehead in exasperation.

"You're a very irritating girl, and I'm not talking to you," huffed Stubbs, folding his arms and hunkering down on his gatepost.

"And me. What he said," echoed Montgomery, crouching back on his perch.

"You two are so annoying!" shouted Cay. Out of the corner of her eye, she saw a dark shape moving slowly away from her across the vicarage lawn. "Well, if you won't tell me, I bet Elgar will," she cried. Without waiting for an answer, she sped off across the grass.

The gargoyles craned their heads round to watch Cay as she ran to intercept the cat.

Montgomery sighed. "This is not going to end well, Mr. Stubbs."

"Not end well at all, Mr. Montgomery," agreed Stubbs.

Elgar was having a pleasant morning stroll around the vicarage grounds when he felt the lawn begin to shake under his paws.

What the—? He didn't have time to finish the thought before Cay snatched him up, plunked him over her shoulder, and began to spin round like a top.

"What are you doing?" hissed Elgar, hanging on with all the strength his paws could muster.

"We had a new arrival last night, didn't we? A boy. Don't you dare try to deny it!" said Cay.

"Put me down!" pleaded Elgar. "Grimm said he'd have me stuffed and mounted if I said anything."

"Aha!" cried Cay. "So it's a conspiracy!"

"I'm warning you," moaned Elgar.

"Who is he?" shouted Cay. "Where did he come from?"

"Too late," Elgar said, and he promptly threw up down the back of Cay's T-shirt.

"Ew," she groaned, unceremoniously dropping Elgar onto the front lawn. "That's revolting!"

"You're lucky I didn't bite off your arm, you lunatic brat!" said the cat, trying to regain his sense of balance. "I'd only just had that kipper. Now I'll have to wait until dinner, and that's hours away." With a theatrical sniff and flick of his tail, he stalked off unsteadily across the grass.

Wrinkling her nose at the smell wafting from her clothes, Cay decided to go home and change before pursuing her investigations. The gargoyles chuckled as she ran past, and Stubbs took great delight in shouting out, "Whiffy, whiffy, cat-sick girl," much to Montgomery's amusement.

Some ten minutes later, a freshly laundered Cay emerged from her house and sprinted back toward the vicarage, only to see Gabriel walking just ahead of her.

"Gabriel, Gabriel!" she shouted. "Wait up!"

The angel turned to look at her, a smile on his face. "Good morning, Miss Forrester," he said. "And why are you in such a hurry?"

"It's a conspiracy!" she pouted.

"What is?"

"I know there's a boy at the vicarage, as I saw Grimm carrying him there last night, but Monty and Stubbs refuse to say anything, and Elgar threw up down my back. It's not been a good morning so far."

Gabriel sniffed. "Yes, you do carry the faint aroma of kippers, and since it seems pointless to say otherwise, yes, there is a boy at the vicarage. I found him in the churchyard last night. He had a head injury and was unconscious, so I asked Grimm and Ignatius to tend to his wounds and look after him. I also asked the gargoyles and Elgar not to say anything, as I'd rather nobody made a fuss. Does that shoot down your conspiracy theory?"

"Crashed and burned," said Cay. "Still, it is very exciting. Perhaps I can teach him how to fly my kite?"

"I'm sure when he wakes up he would like a new friend," said Gabriel.

"When will that be?" asked Cay.

"Not for a few days yet, I should think. He did look badly hurt, but he has Grimm looking after him, so he's in very good hands."

Cay beamed, then changed the subject. "Oh, Gabriel, you haven't forgotten my birthday, have you? I'm going to be eleven, you know!"

"Your birthday's not for three weeks," Gabriel reminded her.

"It's close enough. You haven't forgotten, have you?"

"No, I haven't forgotten," chuckled Gabriel. "There's something special for you on my workbench."

Cay clapped her hands together. "Brilliant. What is it?"

"I'm old, Cay, not daft." He put an arm round her shoulders. "Come on, then, let's show you our new arrival or you'll end up exploding with curiosity."

Cay looked at Jonathan as he lay, pale and still, tucked up in bed in the vicarage guest room. Behind his right ear, a wad of gauze held in place with a bandage covered what Grimm had called "a nasty scalp wound."

"I wonder who he is," said Cay.

"Dunno," said Elgar, perching on the end of the bed near Jonathan's feet. "Turning up in the churchyard in the middle of the night. All very mysterious, I must say."

"I wonder why."

"How do you mean?" asked Elgar.

"Well, people usually come to Hobbes End because they need help, to be somewhere safe, yeah?"

The cat nodded.

"So why is *he* here? What help does he need?"

"We can ask him when he wakes up," said Elgar.

"Do you think it's going to freak him out?" asked Cay.

"What, me? I'm a talking cat. What's not to like?"

Cay raised her eyebrows. "I don't think they have talking cats anywhere else. Or angels, or gargoyles like Monty and Stubbs, or villages with minds of their own."

"Or werewolves?" Elgar stared at Cay.

"Well, I wasn't going to open with that one," said Cay a touch defensively. "I thought I might start off with 'Hello, my name's Cay, what's yours?'"

"Probably a good idea," said Elgar. "I have a feeling that whoever he is, he's in for an interesting stay. Right, then, cup of tea?"

"Don't mind if I do," said Cay. She followed Elgar to the door but stopped and gave the new arrival a backward glance. "Wake up soon, strange boy," she said quietly. "I'm lonely."

The only reply she received was the gentle susurration of Jonathan's shallow breathing.

Chapter 4

FEVER DREAMS

Jonathan slowly opened his eyes, the pain in his head ebbing and flowing like waves on a beach. He was soaked in sweat, his whole body trembling, and he was lying in a strange bed in a strange room, with moonlight filtering through a crack in the curtains.

Reaching up, he found a gauze pad attached to the base of his skull with a bandage. Even the memory of his injury, the sensation of shifting bone, made him feel sick. And then he remembered how he had gotten the injury—snatches of memories drifting across his awareness—and he felt sicker still . . .

He tried to sit up, but the room tilted crazily about him and he slumped back against the pillows. A distant panic began to fill him; all he could think about was getting to the pile of rubble that had poured into the cellar, so he could dig out his father. If he didn't dig, then his father could die. He had to get back.

Forcing himself upright, he swung his legs out of bed and placed his bare feet on the floor. He noticed that he was wearing pajamas, but he had no idea where they'd come from. Shuffling to the door, he opened it to reveal a landing with other doors leading off it and stairs leading down. Bracing himself against the wall, he slowly and painfully made his way along the landing, down the stairs, and along a stone-floored hallway to what looked like a front door.

There was a key in the lock. He turned it, and with a muffled click the bolt slid back into its housing. Jonathan opened the door and edged forward to brace himself on the frame. He didn't recognize what he saw. A wide lawn was split by a long gravel drive, leading down to a pair of open gates. Beyond the gates he could see something glinting from inside a low-hanging mist, but his vision wouldn't stay focused long enough for him to figure out what it was.

Cool night air brushed his skin, and he shivered as the sweat that continued to pour from him turned to pinpricks of ice. A voice at the back of his head told him that this was stupid, that he was hurt, that he had no idea where he was or where he was going, but he ignored it. Every time he shut his eyes he saw his father mouthing *go* at him before the avalanche of bricks and wood slammed downward.

"I'm ... coming ... Dad," Jonathan gasped as he took faltering, barefoot steps onto the gravel of the drive. It crunched quietly beneath his feet, but he didn't hear it. He just concentrated on putting one foot in front of the other without giving in to the spinning world around him. As he passed through the open gates he thought he heard voices calling out to him from somewhere up above, but he ignored them.

Looking to his left, he saw a road leading toward a church and a cluster of cottages; to his right, the road disappeared off into a wall of trees. It was this route he chose as he remembered the car driving on leaves and branches, remembered his mother half carrying him through a forest. Where was his mother now? Surely it was this road that would take him home, back to where she'd be waiting for him.

He staggered onward, the material of his pajamas sticking to his skin. He couldn't understand how he could feel so hot and so cold at the same time. Just as he passed beneath the trees, he felt sure he could hear voices again, muttering now from somewhere behind him.

The pain made it difficult to think, but disjointed

fragments of his memory slowly pulled themselves closer together to form a coherent and frightening whole. It's those monsters, he thought to himself with a horrified shudder. The ones in bowler hats. I can't let them find me.

He increased his speed, lurching along the unmade road with barely enough control to stay upright. Stones cut his feet, branches reached out to catch his face, but all he could think about was getting home, saving his dad — who would have miraculously avoided the worst of the falling masonry. And his mom would be there too, cooking dinner — he could have fish and chips to make up for the meal he'd had to leave behind.

Gasping for breath and with his head screaming at him in agony, Jonathan shuffled round a bend in the road to step into a patch of bright moonlight. In front of him lay a village with a church, a green, a cluster of cottages, and a pond glinting beneath a layer of mist. Jonathan stopped, and with hysterical laughter bubbling up inside him he sank to his knees and keeled over. He'd turned himself round somehow, and he was back where he started.

Standing in the road not three meters away were the silhouettes of two figures, one burly, one slim. Had he walked right back to the monsters? The huge figure dashed forward, and Jonathan braced himself for the death he felt sure was coming. The pain in his head grew unbearable, and hot tears ran down his face.

Hands reached for him and he shut his eyes. He barely heard Grimm's rumbling baritone, asking him if he was all right, before the huge man gently picked him up and cradled him to his chest.

"Dad?" Jonathan mumbled.

"No, lad," said Grimm, an odd catch in his voice. "Not your dad, but you're safe here, you're safe. Nobody will hurt you or my name's not Halcyon Grimm."

"Where . . . am . . . I?" begged Jonathan as he clung to Grimm, the ground seeming to fly by beneath him.

"You're home," said Ignatius, his face taut with worry as he strode along next to them. "You're home."

"Home . . ." Jonathan sighed. Then he blacked out again.

Chapter 5

FAR FROM ORDINARY

The sound of church bells gradually filtered through Jonathan's fuzzy head. Sunlight brushed his face, and he could feel something cold and metallic being pressed against his chest. Slowly opening his eyes, he saw a huge man with a bald head and a stethoscope plugged into his ears.

Jonathan froze.

Grimm looked down to see a frightened Jonathan staring at him. "I wondered why your heart suddenly went into overdrive," he said, unclipping the stethoscope and placing it carefully in an old leather doctor's bag. "Don't be afraid. My name's Grimm, and I've been keeping a very close eye on you since you arrived. Now,

I know you're probably scared and you're not going to believe anything I say, but you're safe, and you're among friends, truly."

Jonathan tried to sit up, but pain lanced through his head. He fell back against the pillows and bit his lip against the dull, red ache that spread behind his eyes.

"*Whoa!* Don't move your head so quickly. You're recovering from a fractured skull. If we hadn't found you when we did, we wouldn't be having this conversation."

"Where am I?" Jonathan asked through gritted teeth.

"You're in the village of Hobbes End," said Grimm. "Specifically, you're in one of the spare bedrooms of the vicarage in the village of Hobbes End. Those bells you can hear are from the church next door. St. Michael's. If you listen closely, you can tell that the bell ringers need substantial practice if they're to stop sounding like an explosion in a saucepan factory."

Jonathan couldn't help but give Grimm a weak smile.

"What's your name, son?" asked Grimm.

"It's Jonathan."

"Then I'm pleased to meet you, Jonathan," said Grimm, smiling broadly to reveal a set of even white teeth, quite out of keeping with the battered condition of the rest of his face. "Do you know how you got here?"

Jonathan frowned as he tried to make sense of what

had happened. But the man had said he was safe . . . Perhaps he could help Dad, too?

"The cottage! Dad! Those . . . things! Mom pulled me out, and we got into the car and . . ." Jonathan put his hand to his forehead. Everything after that was mostly a blur. But he knew he had one important question. "Is Mom here?" he asked, fighting back the tears that threatened to spill down his face.

Grimm shook his head. "You've been here a week, lad. We found you in the churchyard. You were unconscious and sporting a nasty head wound. There was nobody else about."

"But Mom put me in the car . . . Why would she just leave me here?" Jonathan cried. "I need to go find out what happened to Dad, too. He could be hurt." Unable to lock it away any longer, he put his head in his hands and sobbed. A week? How could his dad have survived a week in all that rubble?

Grimm placed a huge, reassuring hand on Jonathan's shoulder and let him cry. With tears filling his eyes, Jonathan was unable to see the look of anguish on Grimm's face — the big man was distraught as a result of lying to the new arrival.

"Look, Jonathan," he said at last, "we're going to help you, it's what we do here. Hobbes End is a safe place, and

I guess your mother must have known that — it must be why she brought you here. You mentioned something about a cottage and your dad?"

Jonathan nodded, and Grimm handed him a tissue to wipe his eyes and nose.

"Well," said Grimm. "I can help with that. You aren't going anywhere farther than the bathroom for another week, so how about you give me the address you were living at, and I'll go and take a look for you?"

Jonathan gave Grimm a sad smile. "Thank you," he said, relieved that someone seemed to believe him and was going to help.

"Right," said Grimm. "I'm going to get you a mug of tea first. Ignatius will be back from Sunday service in a bit, so you can sit and have a chat with him."

"Who's Ignatius?" asked Jonathan.

"He's the vicar of Hobbes End," said Grimm. "You'll like him. Now just relax and try not to wave your head about. I'll be back in a bit."

Jonathan nodded and watched Grimm leave the room, then turned his head to look at the open window. Sunlight poured in, and a gentle breeze ruffled the curtains. He could hear the sounds of people from outside: murmurs, the odd car engine, and a girl's laughter. Suddenly feeling horribly alone, he decided to disobey Grimm and take a look at the world outside. He sat up, swung his legs out of bed, waited for the room to stop spinning, and tottered to the window.

Shielding his eyes against the sun, he could see gardens surrounded by a high stone wall, and a long gravel drive leading to some open gates—it looked familiar somehow. Beyond the gates lay a village green flanked by thatched cottages, a huge pond, and a forest that stretched as far as the eye could see. People were walking to and fro, and over on the far side of the green, beyond a row of beech trees, was a village shop with a bench of fresh fruit and vegetables propped up outside.

He heard another shriek of laughter, and Jonathan saw that it came from a girl being chased around the green by a large black cat. The cat kept catching her, jumping up onto her back, and looking as though he was trying to be sick. He'd then jump off and they'd start all over again.

Jonathan pressed his hand against the glass. It had been such a long time since he'd had any proper friends—he'd moved house so often that he'd never had time really to get to know anyone. He doubted he'd be here long enough to make friends with the girl, whoever she was.

He was about to climb back into bed when he saw the two gargoyles on the gates turn round and wave at him. Jonathan reached out and shut the curtains before gingerly touching the gauze pad that was taped to the back of his head.

I'm going nuts, he thought to himself. *I've got brain damage.*

But he had to look again. He opened the curtains a crack. The gargoyles were still there, smiling and waving. He stifled a hysterical giggle and shuffled backwards to sit on the bed, his mind in a whirl. Just then, he heard footsteps on the stairs, and a tall, thin man in a tweed suit, blue shirt, clerical collar, and wire-rimmed glasses strode into the room, bearing a mug of tea.

"Hello, Jonathan," said the man. "I'm Ignatius Crumb, vicar of Hobbes End. Are you all right? You look a bit pale. Did Grimm say it was okay for you to be up and about?"

Jonathan just stared at Ignatius and pointed toward the window. "Gargoyles" was all he could say.

"Oh dear," sighed Ignatius. "I thought we might have more time." He seemed unsure as to what to do next.

"Is that tea for me?" asked Jonathan.

"Oh, yes," said Ignatius. "Have a sip; it'll make you feel much better."

Jonathan nodded, took the tea, and proceeded to do just that.

As Ignatius sat down next to him on the bed, Jonathan noticed that he had a streak of white in his hair, running back from his temple like a scar. The vicar took an unlit pipe from his shirt pocket and toyed with it nervously.

"It's like this," he said, turning to face Jonathan. "Hobbes End is not an ordinary village; in fact, it's far from ordinary."

Jonathan just stared at him.

"Oh dear," Ignatius said again. "I'm not very good at this, am I?" He paused. "Tell you what — wait there a minute."

Jonathan watched as Ignatius bolted from the room and thundered down the stairs. There was the noise of a door banging open, footsteps on gravel, and a cry of *"Cay!"* from outside in the garden. There followed some semiaudible mutterings, and then a much lighter set of footsteps came back up the stairs. Jonathan gripped his mug tightly and waited to see who it was going to be.

A mass of auburn hair peeped round the doorway; beneath it was a pretty, freckled face with hazel eyes and a quirky grin. It was the girl Jonathan had seen being chased by the cat.

"Hello, strange boy," she said, her smile making Jonathan beam at her in return. "I'm Cay, and I gather you may have broken your brain."

"They've been nattering for ages," said Grimm. "I suppose that's a good thing?"

Ignatius nodded. "Cay's doing a better job than me. I can stand in front of a congregation and relay something topical yet interesting for a sermon, and yet the second I'm asked a question about Monty and Stubbs, I dry up. Why is that?"

Grimm chuckled to himself. "He caught you on the hop, that's all. What bothers me is having to lie to him and everyone else about how he came here. He was so upset when he thought his mother had just abandoned him. He told me what he remembered, and I managed to reassure him by saying I'd go and take a look at the cottage and make sure his dad isn't trapped in the rubble."

"That was the right thing to do," said Ignatius. "If only we could have told Jonathan that you'd already been out there and found nothing. It might have been of some comfort to him."

"Hmm," said Grimm. "I hope his parents turn up sooner rather than later. It's their choice to tell him the truth or not, but we can't keep it from him indefinitely. I can't watch the lad suffer in ignorance."

"I know," said Ignatius. "But we'll have to let Gabriel decide that."

"How is he?" asked Grimm.

"I've barely seen him," said Ignatius. "Since he left Jonathan with us, he's just kept to his cottage—he didn't even come to the service this morning. I guess he's trying not to fret about Darriel and Savantha and that he's heard nothing from either of them for a week now."

"Nothing at all?" asked Grimm.

Ignatius shook his head. "They've just disappeared. I hope it's because they're hiding somewhere until they think it's safe enough to come and get Jonathan. Or they may be trying to petition Lucifer for help. I guess Gabriel's worried about what Belial will do if he captures one or both of them."

"Do you think they'd tell Belial where Jonathan is hidden?"

"He's an archdemon, Grimm. I don't want to think about what he'd do to get the information."

"What did you tell the rest of the villagers?"

"The same story we told Jonathan. That we found him in the graveyard and that we don't know where he's from."

"More lies," said Grimm, shaking his head.

"I know," said Ignatius. "But it's necessary. At least I can trust everyone in the village not to mention

Jonathan's arrival to anyone outside Hobbes End. If there's one thing we're good at, it's keeping secrets."

"So, let me get this straight," said Jonathan. "Hobbes End is this ancient little village in the middle of a forest, and it has a *soul*."

Cay nodded. "Well, that's how Gabriel describes it. It's like it has a personality."

"And how did this happen?"

"Well, when Gabriel got exiled from Heaven, this is where he landed, right in the middle of the pond. All the power from his wings soaked into the earth, and over the years Hobbes End developed a mind of its own."

"So Gabriel is an angel? And he's living here, in Hobbes End?"

"Was," said Cay. "He's retired. He builds clocks now, and he's very good at it too. He's been here since . . . 1666, I think."

"Right," said Jonathan.

"Oh," said Cay, waving a finger for emphasis, "and the village calls out to people who need help, who need somewhere to be safe. That's who all the villagers are. They're people who have come here because they need to hide from something or someone. I think there are about eighty people here at the moment — well, eighty-one if we count you." She grinned.

Jonathan rubbed his face; the painkillers Grimm had given him were beginning to wear off, and he could feel the onset of another terrific headache.

"What's to stop anyone from just walking into Hobbes End to find them when they feel like it? What's the village going to do about that?" he asked, his tone betraying that he didn't believe a word Cay was saying.

"Oh, if the village didn't want someone to wander in, it would just turn them round and send them back out. They'd never get anywhere near the place. Like I said, the village is very protective of the people who live in it. Anything evil that tried to get in would catch fire. Well, that's the theory — never seen it happen myself. For example, when you tried to walk out the other night —"

"I what?" said Jonathan. And then the memories began to flicker back — his bare feet on the gravel, the green, Grimm picking him up . . .

"You were delirious and had a fever," said Cay. "You wandered out of the house in the middle of the night, and the village thought you were trying to leave. It knew you were hurt and that it wasn't safe for you to be wandering around in the dark, so it turned you round and sent you straight back."

Jonathan shook his head. "Funny, that's really funny," he said.

"But I—"

"No, really," said Jonathan, his tone frosty. "I get a fractured skull when my house collapses on me, I somehow end up here, my mom and dad have disappeared, and I'm having hallucinations of waving gargoyles because I really have broken my brain! Then you come up with this fairy tale of angels and magical villages, and I'm supposed to believe it. I've got a head injury, I'm not mental!"

"Oh," said Cay, looking crestfallen. "I was just trying to help."

Jonathan knew he shouldn't snap at Cay, but he just couldn't stop himself. He really liked her, but what she was saying made him feel like he was the target of some huge joke.

"If you want to help me, then stop making up stories," he said.

"I see," said Cay, sounding quite composed, as if she'd expected Jonathan to react the way he had. "Then I guess if I'm going to make you understand, I'll have to bring out the big guns." She got up and put her head round the bedroom door. "Elgar!" she called out. "Some help in here, please."

Jonathan watched as a thundering on the stairs turned into the large black cat with white front paws. Elgar jumped onto the bed and stalked up to the bemused boy until his face was barely inches away, his whiskers twitching, his yellow eyes boring into Jonathan's. The cat held the pose for a good twenty seconds before biting Jonathan gently on the nose.

"Ow!" cried Jonathan, clapping his hands to his face.

"Hallucinate that!" said Elgar.

Jonathan stared at the cat in horrified curiosity. "It . . . it . . ."

"Yes, *it* talks," said Elgar. "And I have a name, you know."

Jonathan looked wide-eyed at Cay. She just shrugged and smiled.

"What you have to ask yourself, Sonny Jim," Elgar said to Jonathan, "is the following. Have I actually gone stark, raving hat stand? Or has everything Cay said to me so far been incredible but true?"

Jonathan just stared at the cat, his mouth open.

"Oh," said Elgar. "The gargoyles, Monty and Stubbs, are quite hurt that you didn't wave back to them earlier on. They're simple souls, but that's no reason to take advantage of their good nature. Now shuffle over to the window and wave at them, or else!"

Too astonished to argue, Jonathan slowly got out of bed and walked to the window. Opening the curtains, he saw the two gargoyles looking up at him expectantly. Feeling slightly ridiculous, he raised a hand and waved at them. Obviously overjoyed, the two gargoyles not only waved back but did a synchronized jig on their respective gateposts.

"Pop yourself back into bed, then," said Elgar, smiling like a Cheshire cat. "It's time we began your Hobbes End education."

Chapter 6

BOGEYMEN

Oh, Darriel, you've been so stubborn. Look at what we've had to do to your wings."

An angel, bound in chains, hung from a hook on the ceiling. Apart from the illumination of a single overhead bulb, all around him was darkness. At his feet lay a pile of blood and feathers. The angel's head lolled on his chest; his body sagged in exhaustion.

"No pithy retort, no defiant response?" said a chilling voice from outside the narrow circle of light.

The angel mumbled something, the words so mangled and quiet as to be inaudible.

"Speak up, then. Tell me what I want to hear and all this unpleasantness will stop. Where . . . is . . . your son, Jonathan?"

Darriel's lips moved, but no sound came out.

"Please don't make me step in all that mess," said the voice. "I have new shoes."

Darriel just moaned.

There was the sound of footsteps on stone, and a figure appeared out of the gloom. A tall, cadaverous man studied the wounded angel through dark, glittering eyes set deep in their sockets. The skin on his face was yellow and thin; it bulged and rippled as if something beneath was trying to claw its way out. He reached out and lifted Darriel's chin.

"I think Rook is tired of beating you to a pulp," said the man. "Then again, I can just let Crow take over. And when he's finished, there's always Raven."

Darriel's lips moved, and the man leaned in close enough to hear what the angel was trying to say.

"Sorry ... Gabriel," the wounded angel croaked. "Sorry ... Dad." Then he closed his eyes and slipped into blessed unconsciousness.

"Well, well," said the man. "We finally know where the boy is. Pain is such a useful tool for eliciting the truth."

Rook stepped out of the shadows to stand next to his master. "Where do we find him, Belial?" the demon asked hungrily. "Where have they hidden the boy?"

"They've hidden him in Hobbes End." Belial

grinned. "With this battered carcass's father. How very obvious."

"But we can't enter Hobbes End," growled Rook. "We'd be incinerated on the spot. What good does it do us to know where the boy is?"

Belial smiled a truly awful smile. "Actually, I'd been planning on paying our old friend Gabriel a visit anyway, and I have a suspicion I know exactly how to get into Hobbes End. Tell me, Rook," he said, "how do you fancy a trip to the British Museum?"

Chapter 7
ODDLY NORMAL

Jonathan awoke to find a wet nose pressed up against his. He gave a start before realizing that he was being closely scrutinized by Elgar.

"Morning," said the cat.

"Morning," replied Jonathan. "Your breath is awful."

"You cut me to the quick," said Elgar, pretending to be upset. "I'm a cat—what do you expect my breath to smell like? Potpourri?"

Jonathan grinned.

"Can I have one of those sherbet lemons?" asked Elgar, nodding toward the paper bag that sat on Jonathan's bedside table.

"Yeah," said Jonathan. "It might make you less whiffy."

The cat deftly hooked out one of the boiled sweets and started sucking on it. "Who gave you these?" he asked.

"They were from Mr. and Mrs. Flynn, a nice old couple who live near Cay, apparently."

Elgar rolled his eyes. "Yes, I saw that you'd been getting a steady stream of presents sent up from the inhabitants of our charming little village."

"You're just jealous," said Jonathan.

"Too right I'm jealous," said Elgar. "When *I* turned up, all I got was a preowned dog basket and a chew toy. And what do you get? A stack of get-well cards, sweets, three books, a pile of new clothes, and the loan of Professor Morgenstern's second-best laptop so you can surf the Internet until your brain dissolves."

"Everyone's been really nice," said Jonathan. "Since I've been stuck in here for two weeks now and my head's all healed, Grimm said I could get up and go for a proper walk today. I can meet the villagers and say thank you for the presents."

"Good idea," said Elgar.

"Can I ask you something?" said Jonathan.

"Fire away."

"How is it that you can talk? You're a cat."

"Oh, not that again," said Elgar, heaving a sigh. "It's like I've got an embarrassing skin condition or something. Why can't everyone just let me be myself?" He rubbed a scrunched-up paw in the corner of his eye and pretended to sniffle. He carried on like this for a minute but saw that Jonathan remained unmoved. "You're not going to let this drop, are you?"

Jonathan shook his head.

"Look, if you think me talking is weird, just wait until you find out about Cay's dad's"—Elgar did quote marks with his paws—"condition. I'd tell you myself, but I don't want to spoil the surprise."

Jonathan smiled at the cat as he tried to take everything in. Knowing he wasn't being lied to made a huge difference.

"Like Cay said," continued Elgar, "Hobbes End is a haven for people who need somewhere to be safe. Professor Morgenstern's apparently hiding from MI5 and the CIA. Something about a time machine. Then there's Mrs. Silkwood and her unhealthy obsession with that aspidistra she keeps in her front room. No furniture—just the plant in a big ceramic pot. I assume she's hiding from the men in white coats."

Jonathan snorted with laughter. "You keep telling me about the other villagers. What about you—why are you here?"

"That's a story for another day." Elgar grinned.

"Well, why are you called Elgar? It's an odd name

for a cat. They normally have names like Fluffy or Mittens."

Elgar pretended to be insulted but then ruined it by grinning again. "The day I arrived in Hobbes End, I wandered into the vicarage living room through the open French windows. Ignatius was playing this really sad piece of music on the piano, and when I jumped up onto the piano stool he said, 'Hello, what's your name, then?' I looked at the sheet music he was reading from, read the name of the composer, and said 'Elgar.' Ignatius didn't bat an eyelid, and it's been that way ever since."

"Why didn't you just give him your real name?" asked Jonathan.

"Because I don't like it. I have an awful feeling my parents wanted a girl."

Jonathan laughed so hard, it made his head hurt. "Okay, then, cat. I'll get dressed and see you in the kitchen in a bit."

"Cool," said Elgar. "I'm starving. Don't be long." He jumped to the floor and padded silently from the room.

Jonathan got out of bed, showered, changed into new clothes that Grimm had procured for him, and opened the curtains. He waved at the gargoyles, and as they waved back Jonathan realized that it didn't seem weird anymore. If anything, it felt oddly normal.

This didn't stop him from thinking about his parents

constantly. Grimm had told him that he had visited the destroyed cottage but had found no sign of Jonathan's father or the things that had attacked them. This reassured Jonathan but raised more questions: Where were his parents now? What were those things that had attacked them? And why? Jonathan hoped he wouldn't have to wait too long for the answers.

Leaving his bedroom, he walked down the stairs and past portraits of the previous vicars of Hobbes End. Some looked stern, some looked kind, but all looked as though they were someone to be reckoned with.

Reaching the main hallway, Jonathan was almost deafened by the thunderous cry of *"Tea up!"* He gently pushed open the kitchen door. Over by the butler sink, Grimm was placing a teapot and mugs on a tray. He turned and beamed at Jonathan.

"Guess," he said, holding up the teapot.

"Um . . ." said Jonathan.

"He wants you to guess what tea it is," mumbled Elgar, face-down in a bowl of kippers. "Grimm's got hundreds of different ones, all in little tins in the pantry. Some of them are lovely, but others could strip paint. Very odd hobby for a grown man, I must say."

"Philistine," growled Grimm, flicking one of Elgar's ears with a finger the size of a small banana.

"Ow!" hissed Elgar.

A copy of the *Times* was lowered to reveal the raised eyebrows of Ignatius. "Let the lad sit down, gentlemen, please," he said. He smiled at Jonathan and pulled a chair out for him. "Elgar and Grimm like each other really; they just have a funny way of showing it."

Grimm sighed, plunked the tray of crockery on the table, then went outside to wash his car. If there was one thing Grimm liked more than making tea, gardening, cooking, or cricket, it was washing his prized car — an old Daimler.

Jonathan sat down, and Ignatius poured him a mug of what turned out to be nothing more offensive than Earl Grey.

"How're you feeling?" the vicar asked. "This is your first proper day up and about, so don't overdo it."

"I feel a bit dizzy, but I'm okay, thanks."

Ignatius nodded. "You will remember what I said, won't you? Until your parents turn up, you must treat the village as your home."

Jonathan grinned and nodded. He liked Ignatius; there was something reassuring about him, something kind.

"You mustn't think you're a burden," Ignatius continued. "This is what we do here in Hobbes End; we look after people."

"That's what Cay and Elgar keep telling me," said

Jonathan, sipping his tea. "Do you think that's why I'm here?"

"I don't know yet," Ignatius lied. "But you mustn't worry."

"I'll try not to," said Jonathan. "But it's difficult. I just keep seeing those . . . things attacking us, and then the ceiling caving in. Do you think they were really monsters, or did I imagine it because of my head injury?"

"I think you saw something, Jonathan, and that it scared both you and your parents."

"I guess. Perhaps they were foreign spies or something. Dad would never say what he did when I asked him. He'd just say that it was better I didn't know. If Dad worked for the government, then maybe somebody would want to kidnap him for secret information, or something?"

"It's possible," said Ignatius.

"But how did Mom know how to bring me here?"

Ignatius shook his head. "Again, I don't know, Jonathan. But now you are here, you're not in any danger."

"Thanks. I don't understand why I'm not more frightened than I actually am."

Ignatius fixed his flint gray eyes on Jonathan. "Perhaps it's just because you're very brave?"

Jonathan smiled. It was then that he noticed an article

splashed on the front page of that day's paper. "What's that?" he asked.

Ignatius spread the *Times* out so they could read it clearly:

PUDDING LANE METEORITE STOLEN FROM BRITISH MUSEUM

Whilst the theory that the Great Fire of London was started by a meteorite as opposed to a careless baker is a contentious one, Abelard Flagg, head curator of the British Museum, had been confident that the meteorite would indeed prove to have ignited the fire that destroyed much of London in September 1666. Mr. Flagg is said to be deeply upset following last night's break-in and subsequent theft of the object. Scotland Yard is investigating but has yet to release a statement.

"Tch!" tutted Ignatius. "Is nothing sacred?" Finishing his tea, the vicar of Hobbes End stood up and stretched, his gangly frame towering over the kitchen table. "Right," he said, "I've got some things I need to do. Cay's waiting for you over at her parents' shop. She's so excited about having someone new to introduce to the other villagers, she may just explode. Elgar wants to go too, so have fun and I'll see you later."

Patting Jonathan tenderly on the shoulder, the vicar of Hobbes End walked out of the kitchen. He'd left the paper on the table, and Jonathan couldn't help but look at the article about the stolen meteorite. There was something odd about it, but he couldn't quite figure out what.

His pondering was interrupted when a grinning Elgar jumped up onto the table.

"Well, Johnny-boy," he said, "I have officially finished my breakfast kipper. Ready to meet the neighbors?"

Chapter 8

Old Friends and Bookends

Jonathan walked down the vicarage drive with Elgar by his side. The fuzziness in his head was slowly wearing off, and he felt strangely peaceful.

"Why does Hobbes End feel so much like home?" he asked Elgar. "I've only been here two weeks, but it feels longer."

"It does that to everyone who comes here for more than a couple of days," said the cat. "It wouldn't be much fun if you spent all your time being homesick, would it?"

"I can't explain it," said Jonathan. "It just feels like I know the village somehow."

"Are you sure you had Earl Grey tea this morning and not one of Grimm's more . . . exotic blends?"

Jonathan chuckled. "It doesn't matter," he said. "Where do we go first, then?"

"First we say hello to the gargoyles, then we wander over to see Cay. Hey, guys, I've got someone I want you to meet!"

Despite knowing that the gargoyles were somehow alive, Jonathan still gaped in astonishment as the two squat statues that perched on top of the vicarage gateposts turned round, hopped down to the ground with muffled thumps, and walked over to greet him.

"Good morning, Jonathan," said the gargoyle on the left. "I'm Mr. Montgomery." He held out a granite paw, which Jonathan hesitantly shook. "And my sturdy, angry-looking friend here is Mr. Stubbs."

"I am not sturdy!" growled Stubbs. "I just have big bones." He glared at Jonathan as if daring him to disagree.

"I know it's difficult, Stubbsey, but try to be polite to Jonathan—he's a guest," said Elgar.

"Sorry," mumbled Stubbs, extending his own paw for Jonathan to shake. "I'm just a bit shy, that's all."

"Shy?" choked Elgar. "You're one of the biggest show-offs I've ever met. Even more than me, and that's saying something, I can tell you."

"Mr. Elgar does have a point," said Montgomery, nodding sagely.

"Ooh, you take that back!" barked Stubbs.

"I will not!" huffed Montgomery, putting his paws on his hips and squaring up to his friend.

"You'll take it back or there'll be fisticuffs," warned Stubbs.

"La-la-la, I can't hear you," replied Montgomery, putting his fingers in his ears.

"Right, that's it," said Stubbs, rolling up imaginary sleeves.

"Time to be off," said Elgar, butting Jonathan in the back of the legs. "We need to get out of the danger zone."

Jonathan did as he was told but cast a quick glance over his shoulder just in time to see Stubbs punch Montgomery in the face. An indignant Montgomery returned the favor with gusto, and a toe-to-toe slugging match ensued. It sounded like someone repeatedly dropping a pile of bricks.

"Are they always like that?" asked Jonathan.

"Nah," said Elgar. "They're just excited because there's a new face staying at the vicarage. They'll pummel each other for a few minutes, then either get bored or Grimm will tell them to cut it out and get back to guarding the place. Anyhoo, next on our tour we have the village green."

In front of Jonathan, the residents of Hobbes End wandered to and fro across the wide expanse of grass, enjoying the summer sunshine and bidding each other good morning.

"All very idyllic, isn't it?" said Elgar. "But it's home. Oh, there's Mr. Peters. Let's go say hello."

Jonathan looked along the road to where an elderly man dressed all in black and sporting a wide-brimmed hat and sunglasses was sitting on a bench and peeling an apple.

"Morning, Mr. P.," said Elgar. "This is Jonathan. He's staying at the vicarage for a while."

"Ah, our new arrival," said Mr. Peters, stiffly getting to his feet and shaking Jonathan's hand. "Welcome. I hope you've recovered from your injuries?"

"Yes, thanks."

"Watch out for that girl and her kite, though. She's a menace." He nodded knowingly, sat down, and went back to his apple.

"Okay, I will," said Jonathan, looking perplexed.

"He means Cay," said Elgar as they continued their walk. "Let's get over to the shop before she starts chewing the wallpaper with boredom. Oh, and whatever you do, don't stare at her dad — he doesn't like it."

"Why would I stare at her dad?" asked Jonathan, sounding worried.

"You'll see," said Elgar, a cheeky grin on his face.

They stepped into the village shop just as a thin

woman clutching a packet of plant food came out. The woman took one look at Elgar, scowled, and scurried off toward the church.

"Have I done something wrong?" asked Jonathan.

"Nah," said Elgar. "That's Mrs. Silkwood. You know, the one with the aspidistra? She doesn't like me very much."

"Why?"

"Long story. I'll tell you later."

Jonathan was just about to insist that Elgar tell him the story right then when a thundering of feet came down the back stairs. Seconds later, Cay burst into view from the open doorway behind the counter.

"Hello!" she cried out. "Where've you been? You'd better not have gone anywhere without me." She smiled at Jonathan, the freckles across the bridge of her nose prominent after hours of running around in the sunshine.

"Hi," said Jonathan, suddenly feeling shy for some reason.

"We just saw your mate Mr. Peters," Elgar said to Cay. "He's not happy about you dive-bombing him with your new kite."

"Shhh! Dad'll hear."

"Too late!" growled a voice. A very tall man in shorts and T-shirt loped from the private rooms at the rear of

the shop and vaulted effortlessly over the counter. He had a bushy, silver-black beard and piercing eyes with curious yellow irises. He held his hand out for Jonathan to shake. "Hello, I'm Kenneth Forrester, Cay's dad. Welcome to Hobbes End." He bent to whisper in Jonathan's ear, "You're a godsend; Cay's been driving us nuts having nobody to play with."

Jonathan shook Mr. Forrester's hand but couldn't stop looking at his eyes. They glittered bright yellow, reflecting the light pouring through the shop window.

Elgar coughed politely. "Staring," he reminded Jonathan.

"Oh, um, sorry, hello," stammered Jonathan, also noticing that Mr. Forrester had exceptionally hairy arms.

"Still staring," hissed Elgar.

Mr. Forrester smiled and ruffled Jonathan's hair. "Don't worry," he said. "You'll soon get used to our . . . peculiarities." He turned to Cay. "I'm off for a run. Don't pester your mother, or Mr. Peters for that matter."

Cay tried, and failed, to look innocent.

"Have fun and don't upset anybody." Mr. Forrester sighed, rolling his eyes. The bell on the ceiling jingled and he was gone.

"I'll just go get Mom," Cay said to Jonathan. "She wanted to say hello too." She disappeared into the depths of the cottage, reappearing hand in hand with a woman who looked just like an older version of her daughter. Mrs. Forrester was barely taller than Cay; she had the same auburn hair, hazel eyes, freckles, and quizzical smile. Unlike her daughter, however, Joanne Forrester was silent.

She kissed Jonathan gently on the cheek before standing back and moving her hands in complex patterns in the air.

"Mom says welcome," said Cay, translating her mother's signing. "And that your eyes are incredibly blue."

"Thank you," said Jonathan, wishing he understood sign language.

Mrs. Forrester smiled and reached out, gently touching Jonathan's face. She signed again.

"Mom says not to be afraid," said Cay. "You'll be safe here, and you'll never need to be alone unless you want to."

Jonathan smiled and nodded at Mrs. Forrester. She smiled back, signed briefly to Cay, and after pausing to scratch Elgar behind the ears, disappeared into the rooms behind the shop.

The cat sighed. "I love her."

"Right," said Cay. "Shall we go and see who's about?"

Jonathan nodded, then before he could say anything Cay grabbed his hand and pulled him out of the shop.

"Where first, Elgar?" she asked the cat.

"Hmm, Gabriel, I think. He's coming round for dinner tonight, so it would be good for Jonathan to meet him before then."

"Okey-dokey," replied Cay, striding off toward the church. "We should see Gabriel first anyway. It's, like, respectful, since he made the village in the first place."

"What's up with your dad's eyes?" asked Jonathan, who hadn't been listening.

Cay jerked to a halt. "What do you mean?" she asked, sounding defensive.

"Well, they were this odd yellow color, and they reflected the light and, um . . ."

Cay let him suffer for a moment before grinning and poking him in the ribs. "Dad's the reason we came to Hobbes End," she said. "He's a werewolf. I would have told you earlier, but I wanted you to meet him first. You never know how people are gonna react."

Jonathan stared at her with his mouth agape. He was off to meet an angel—a real *angel*—and now he'd met a werewolf!

"You'll have to forgive my young friend," Elgar said to Cay. "He's having quite a morning."

Cay laughed out loud. "I bet he is," she said. "Come on, let's go see Gabriel. I won't bite!"

Too stunned to say anything, Jonathan followed his

new friends as they strolled through the lych-gate, round the church, and toward a large thatched cottage nestled against the forest's edge.

As they walked, Jonathan noticed that Ignatius was standing quiet and still in the far corner of the churchyard. He had a bunch of white roses in his hand, and he looked sad.

"What's wrong with Ignatius?" whispered Jonathan.

"Oh!" said Cay. "I thought he would have told you himself."

"Told me what?"

"Ignatius's wife and son were killed in a car crash three years ago. He misses them ever so much, and he visits their grave every day. That's where they're buried."

"How old was Ignatius's son?" asked Jonathan, wondering if he should go over and say something.

"David was five," said Elgar. "It hit Ignatius really hard. It's the reason Grimm's staying at the vicarage."

"Why's that?"

"Grimm and Ignatius grew up together here in Hobbes End," said Elgar. "Grimm was serving in the army when he heard of the accident, but he left immediately and came back to look after Ignatius. Three years later, he's still here."

"Old friends and bookends," whispered Cay.

Jonathan looked at her.

"It's what Grimm says sometimes when he thinks nobody's listening," she said.

Jonathan nodded. Lying in bed for two weeks had given him plenty of time to see how Ignatius and Grimm treated each other. Old friends and bookends was exactly what they were.

"C'mon," said Cay. "Don't worry about Ignatius. He'll be okay. Now, let's see if Gabriel's in."

They reached the thatched cottage. Lifting the heavy iron knocker, Cay beat out a lengthy tattoo on the door. There was a brief pause, then a voice from high up called out, "Hello, who is it?" They looked up to see a flustered elderly man leaning out the gable window. "I'm trying to work on your birthday present," he called down to Cay. "If you keep bothering me every ten minutes, it'll never get finished!"

Jonathan, finding himself slightly afraid and not a little in awe, gave a self-conscious wave and said hello. He felt better once he saw that the angel was smiling at him. In fact, he thought to his surprise, Gabriel just looked normal. Though there was *something* about him . . .

"Good morning, young man. I trust you are being well looked after by Miss Forrester and her feline assistant."

"I am not an assistant," sulked Elgar as Cay grinned.

"Yes, thanks, Mr. Gabriel," Jonathan replied. "There's a lot to take in. But it's fun, and Ignatius and Grimm are really nice."

"Good," Gabriel nodded. "Well, I am very busy right now, but I'll be seeing you later for dinner. Oh, you're invited too, Cay."

She beamed at the angel.

Gabriel withdrew his head and made to shut the window, but Jonathan blurted something out. He just couldn't help himself. From the second he'd looked up and seen Gabriel's face and heard his voice, he'd felt this odd sensation of familiarity, and he didn't want to let it go. He had to say something to keep the old man there, so he said the first thing that came into his head.

"Are you really an angel?"

Gabriel paused a moment before looking directly at Jonathan, one set of extraordinarily blue eyes to another. "I was, Jonathan. I was." He didn't say anything else, but just closed the window. As he did so, Jonathan thought that the expression on the angel's face was one of the saddest he could imagine.

"Is he all right?" asked Elgar.

"I don't know," said Cay. "He's been really quiet recently. But come on, loads of people to see. I think you should meet Professor Morgenstern next, and just to warn you, he probably won't be wearing any socks."

Jonathan smiled and let Cay pull him away from Gabriel's cottage. Despite the oddness of Hobbes End and the ever-present worry over his parents' absence, he had difficulty imagining that anywhere else could make him feel so completely at home.

Chapter 9

OMELETS AND ANGELS

Elgar walked back to the vicarage, having accompanied Jonathan and Cay on a marathon door-knocking session that had lasted most of the day. Everyone had been pleased to see that Jonathan was recovering, and he got the chance to say thank you for all the cards and presents he'd received. Full of tea and Battenberg cake, Elgar had left Cay showing Jonathan how to fly her kite.

"A catnap before dinner, I think," he said, pushing his way through the flap in the kitchen door. Once inside, he climbed into a wicker basket that sat in the corner. The basket had once belonged to a little King Charles spaniel, the beloved pet of Ignatius's mother, Constance. Constance had named the spaniel Renoir after her favorite Impressionist painter.

Renoir had passed away many years before, and when Constance left Hobbes End to live in Devon after the death of her husband, Salvador, she left the basket behind in case Ignatius ever decided to get a dog of his own. Ignatius had been considering the pros and cons of a springer spaniel when Elgar had arrived at the vicarage and claimed the vacant basket. After that, Ignatius quickly gave up on the idea of getting a dog.

"Ah, home sweet home." The cat chuckled to himself. "I just wish I could get rid of the smell of wet dog." He stretched, and with a loud crack his back paws punched through the side of the basket.

"Oops!" he exclaimed, surveying the damage.

"What have you done now?" asked Grimm, looking over his shoulder from the other side of the kitchen. Elgar gave him a sheepish grin and began trying desperately to free himself. Watching Elgar as he struggled and swore, Grimm had enormous trouble suppressing a smile.

"Tell you what," he said to the entangled cat. "Hold still and I'll give you a hand." He reached for a meat cleaver hanging to one side of the oven and made a great show of testing its edge with his thumb. Walking over to the basket, he kneeled down and raised the blade. "Don't worry," he said calmly. "You won't feel a thing!"

Not reassured in the slightest, Elgar yowled and sprinted for the door using just his front legs and dragging the basket along with him. He shot through the cat flap, tearing the basket free and sending splintered wicker in all directions. The flap swung to and fro like a saloon door as Grimm laughed his head off.

Ignatius looked into the kitchen to see what all the fuss was about. Seeing Grimm hooting with mirth and clutching a meat cleaver, he decided that he probably didn't want to know.

"Right, then," said the vicar. "I'll go and lay the table for dinner. Jonathan and our guests will be here soon."

"Ah, yes," said Grimm. "It'll be a nice opportunity for Gabriel to see how well Jonathan's settling in and have a chat with him at the same time. When do you think Gabriel will tell him the truth?"

Ignatius shrugged. "Hopefully he won't need to. With any luck Jonathan's parents will return soon and all will be right with the world. I guess at that point we're going to have to apologize to Jonathan for all the deception."

Grimm returned to his omelet making. "Who'd have thought it?" he muttered. "What an interesting summer this is turning out to be."

The front door of the vicarage banged open, and

voices drifted along the hallway. Ignatius, who had just finished laying the dining table, marveled at the ability of children to know precisely when food is about to be served. With a clatter, the heads of Jonathan and Cay — with Elgar at their feet — appeared round the door, closely followed by Gabriel. He was smartly dressed in a black suit, and his long white hair was neatly tied back.

"I found these three outside," he said with a wink. "They looked hungry."

"Dinner's ready!" Grimm bellowed from the kitchen.

"Excellent," said Ignatius. "Grab yourselves a seat."

They all sat down around the oval dining table as Grimm brought in a huge tureen of steaming omelet and peas. Elgar sat on his own chair between Jonathan and Cay, but despite the omelet containing smoked haddock, Grimm just gave him his usual kipper.

"Why don't you want any omelet, Elgar?" asked Cay.

"Have you any idea what that amount of egg would do to my insides?" Elgar replied. "I'd be farting for England!"

"And that is something we can all do without," rumbled Grimm, uncorking a bottle of particularly good wine he'd fetched from the cellar.

"I gather you've been introducing Jonathan to the villagers," Ignatius said to Cay.

She grinned. "Yeah, we saw just about everyone today. Professor Morgenstern had the blueprints for his time machine laid out on his front lawn."

"He'd lost his favorite pen, and he wasn't wearing any socks or shoes," added Jonathan. "I did remember to thank him for lending me his laptop, though. What did he call the thingy that makes his time machine work?" he asked Elgar.

"Reticulate paradox theory," mumbled Elgar through a mouthful of kipper.

"Hmm," said Grimm. "I have no idea whether he really is a genius or just unhinged."

"And then we saw the twins," said Cay. "They showed Jonathan their stuffed-owl collection."

"Ew," Grimm shuddered.

"You're not scared of owls, are you?" asked Elgar.

"I'm not scared of anything!" barked Grimm. "It's just those huge eyes and the way their heads swivel the whole way round so they're looking backwards. It's not natural."

Elgar snorted into his bowl, sending bits of fish everywhere.

"Clara and Cecily do like their taxidermy," said Ignatius. "Although the local owl population seems rather thin on the ground since they arrived."

"Why did they come to Hobbes End?" asked Jonathan.

"I'm not at liberty to divulge that," said Ignatius, trying to suppress a grin. "Everyone is allowed their secrets."

"Oh, I saw Mr. Peters earlier too," said Jonathan. "He seems nice enough, but he doesn't seem very fond of Cay."

Cay pretended to be very interested in the contents of her omelet.

"That's because Cay thinks Mr. Peters is a vampire," said Ignatius. "Which is, of course, nonsense; Mr. Peters is just very sensitive to sunlight—hence the black coat, hat, gloves, and sunglasses. If she was nice to him for a day, she might even notice his patently fangless smile."

"You didn't tell me that," Jonathan said to Cay.

"Well," said an embarrassed Cay, "it's just a theory."

"Think about it, Cay," said Ignatius. "I wish you'd stop trying to knock off his hat with your kite to see if he catches fire, or sneaking up on him in the dark and shoving an ultraviolet flashlight in his face. He bends my ear about it every chance he gets. And Lord knows what he says to your parents . . ."

Cay pouted.

"Who else did you see, Jonathan?" asked Grimm.

"We had tea with Mr. and Mrs. Flynn, and I thanked them for the sherbet lemons."

"They are mighty fine boiled sweets," purred Elgar.

"And then there was Mrs. Silkwood," Jonathan continued. "All she had in her front room was a table with this big green plant in a pot. She wouldn't let us near it, and she refused to let Elgar in the house at all."

"Hmm, she is very protective of her aspidistra," said Ignatius. "And I gather there's a very good reason she won't let Elgar in."

The cat chuckled to himself. "Well, she locked me in her house by accident once. I was stuck in there all morning, and I was busting for a pee."

"Oh, you didn't!" said Grimm. "It's a wonder the poor plant's still alive."

The cat shrugged and continued eating his fish.

Jonathan stole a glance at Gabriel. The feeling of having met him before was stronger than ever, but he knew that was impossible. He'd never even heard of Hobbes End before two weeks ago — and he certainly wouldn't have believed that angels existed. Gabriel sensed he was being watched and met Jonathan's gaze. He smiled.

"Is my birthday present ready?" asked Cay.

Gabriel rolled his eyes in mock annoyance. "It's sitting on my workbench as we speak. And no, I'm not telling you what it is, and no, you can't have it until Sunday."

"But that's five days away," she protested.

"Life can be so unfair." Gabriel grinned.

"Is it true?" asked Jonathan, remembering what Cay had said to him about Gabriel, and dying to know more. "Did you land here after being exiled from Heaven, and did it make the village come alive or something?"

"Oh, this is an amazing story," said Cay.

"I'm glad you find my fall from grace so exciting, Miss Forrester," said Gabriel, pretending to be offended.

"I didn't mean to—"

"It's fine," said the angel. "I'm just teasing you. This story is village legend, so it's only fair that Jonathan know it too. Would you like to hear it?" he asked.

Jonathan nodded and leaned forward.

"Well," said Gabriel. "While we digest that splendid omelet, here is my tale. A long, long time ago—"

"In a galaxy far, far away," mumbled Elgar.

Grimm flicked the cat's ear. "Hush!"

"Heaven was at war with itself. Lucifer, the strongest, brightest, and proudest angel, decided that he knew best as far as creation was concerned. He wanted to rule Heaven his way, and being so proud, he believed himself right. War followed. Brother against brother, sister against sister. In the end Heaven, under the banner of archangel Uriel, managed to stop Lucifer, bind him with chains of glass, and exile him. He fell all the way down to Hell itself, leaving a shattered city behind him. Sadly Uriel then died of his wounds, so Heaven needed someone new to be in charge."

Gabriel took a sip of wine and paused. Jonathan could see that telling this story was difficult for him, and began to wish that he hadn't brought the subject up. Staring into his wineglass, Gabriel continued.

"And so four new angels were created to take care of Heaven.

"My elder brother, Raphael Executor, whose job it was to be just, to be fair, and to rule.

"My big sister, Sammael Morningstar, who lit the stars in the sky to bring light to the void.

"Me, Gabriel Artificer, the engineer with knowledge of how creation worked and how to fix it when it broke.

"And finally, my little brother, Michael Hellbane, the brave soldier, always first into battle and utterly fearless. The four of us brought order and peace for a time, but it didn't last."

"Lucifer?" asked Jonathan.

Gabriel nodded. "Our predecessor wasn't going to just give up. He was powerful, and he wanted revenge. He reigned over a big part of Hell, leaving the rest to be fought over by three archdemons—Belial, Baal, and Lilith."

At the mention of the name Belial, a sudden blend

of anger and fear welled up inside Jonathan. His palms felt clammy, and his shoulders ached, just like they had when the cottage had been attacked. Jonathan jumped when Gabriel touched him on the arm.

"Are you all right?" he asked.

Jonathan nodded, not wanting to spoil Gabriel's story. He took a sip of water and forced himself to appear calm. "Sorry," he said. "I just felt a bit dizzy."

"You're probably tired after being in bed for so long before today. Would you like me to continue another time?"

"No, please don't stop," said Jonathan. "I really want to hear it."

"Okay, then. Using threats and promises, Lucifer joined forces with the archdemons and launched an all-out attack on Heaven. We knew it was coming and we had prepared, but the cost would be dear. We faced the hordes of Hell on the plain of Armageddon—a tiny force of angels against unimaginable odds. We all did . . . questionable things that day." Gabriel sighed. "I had created machines to help us in our fight. The cherubim they were called, my three hollow angels, engines of living metal with wings of razor-edged glass. I remember watching them scythe into the ranks of demons." He paused, sadness evident in his eyes as he continued softly, "I did not think there was that much blood in all of creation."

Gabriel bowed his head a moment, then continued.

"The slaughter was terrible. Angels and demons may be long lived, but we are far from immortal. We can all bleed, we can all die. In the end, even Lucifer was sickened by it. Possibly because some vestige of the angel he had been remained inside him, he decided to stop the fighting and to challenge my sister, Sammael, to a duel. The winner would decide the fate of Heaven and Hell. Michael wanted to fight Lucifer, but he'd been badly wounded, as had I and Raphael. There was just our sister left unscathed, and she was magnificent. She earned her title of Morningstar a thousand times over that day, so bright did she shine as she fought Lucifer.

"And then suddenly, amazingly, she won, and Lucifer, kneeling on the ground at her feet, surrendered. She ordered that from that day forth Heaven and Hell would never again go to war with each other. Angels and demons would be allowed to walk the earth, as long as they masked their true forms and did not interfere with humanity in any way. The archdemons were furious— they wanted to continue the fight, but they were scared of Lucifer and of what he could do, so they went back to Hell, nursing their grudges against him and against

Heaven. Our struggle was almost over, but there was one more tragedy to come."

So powerful was Gabriel's storytelling that Jonathan felt himself transported to the battlefield. He imagined himself standing among the wounded and the dying, adrift in a sea of crimson mud. It was awful.

"It was Raphael's screaming that shattered the silence," said Gabriel. "We found him cradling the body of his wife, his beloved Bethesda, the broken shaft of an arrow sticking out of her throat. We tried to console him, but it was no use. Something inside him broke that day. Instead of being just and kind, he became vengeful and bitter. He ranted at Sammael for not finishing the fight, for not killing Lucifer and the archdemons, for letting them all go home when his wife was dead in his arms. He seemed to forget that I'd lost my own wife in a previous battle. We'd each lost people we loved during the years of war, but all we wanted now was for it to stop."

Gabriel took a deep breath as if the telling of the tale caused him physical pain. The knuckles of his right hand showed white as they gripped his wineglass far too tightly.

"And so we come to the end of my story. Heaven was never the same again, not really. We had all been changed by the horror of war, and the home that we'd fought for seemed darker somehow. The anger inside Raphael grew, and we just stood and watched. We didn't know what else to do; we had no more stomach for fighting. I packed away my cherubim and prayed that I would never see them again. I buried myself in building clocks—the simplicity of their mechanisms reminded me of how creation should be: ordered, regular, predictable. Raphael retreated into his tower, Michael rested to recover from his wounds, and Sammael continued her job of igniting suns.

"Then, one awful day, there was an accident. Just as Sammael started the chain reaction to create a newborn star, Michael suddenly appeared at her side, spear in hand. She said he looked afraid, as if he was expecting an attack, as if he'd been told that she needed saving. She didn't. Sammael could do nothing except watch the awful look on Michael's face as he realized what was happening. He turned to flee, but it was too late. The blast vaporized him, spread his atoms among the stars, and all my sister could do was watch. She's special, you see: she's immune to the heat and radiation of a star; the rest of us are not."

Gabriel's wineglass finally cracked under the pressure of his fingers; murmuring an apology, he set it carefully upon the table.

"Sammael was in shock. She didn't defend herself

as Raphael ordered that for killing her brother she be cast out of Heaven. She wasn't sentenced to Hell as Lucifer had been, but she was to be exiled, never to walk through the gates of Heaven again.

"I watched my sister as she fell, knowing that my time was over too, and I told Raphael that he was no longer my brother. A darkness had taken root in his soul and I could not stand by and watch him turn our home into his own version of Hell. I've always wondered whether he had something to do with the accident that killed Michael, but even now I cannot understand why he would do such a thing.

"Raphael ordered me thrown down after Sammael, but I would not submit to such indignity. I threw myself from the gates of Heaven and let my wings burn as I fell. I no longer wanted to be an angel; I just wanted to be Gabriel and to be left alone. So on the second of September 1666 I crash-landed here, in a little hamlet in the middle of a forest. My wings were badly damaged, and I gave most of what power remained in them to the village itself, to give it life, to make a refuge for me and for anyone who wanted somewhere to be safe. Heaven and Hell would know where I was, but I would not be a threat—I would just be a clock maker—and angels and demons would leave me alone. And with the loss of so much power I began to age much faster than my siblings, become frailer. Still, when I look out my window and see the refuge this village has become, I know it was a price worth paying. And so the years passed and here we are." He shrugged self-consciously and smiled at Jonathan. "Does that answer your question?"

"I . . ." Jonathan stammered, not knowing what to say.

"What happened to Sammael, and to Raphael?" asked Cay.

"Sammael found her way to Hobbes End and stayed for a time, but she could never forgive herself for killing Michael. I tried to tell her my suspicions about Raphael's involvement in Michael's death, but she wouldn't listen—the very idea was so awful, she didn't want even to think about it. We argued a lot, and eventually she left to try to find some peace while walking the earth. I haven't heard from her for many years. As for Raphael, I never heard from him again. The gates of Heaven have been locked shut, and I have no idea what's going on behind them." Gabriel pushed his chair back and stood up. "Please forgive me, but I'm rather tired. I'm going to have to skip dessert. I'll replace the wineglass." He walked to the door, but as he drew level with Jonathan he paused. "I'm sorry for what you've suffered, Jonathan," said the angel. "And I'm sorry for being so preoccupied since you arrived. I meant to give you this earlier today."

Jonathan turned to see Gabriel take off his wristwatch and hold it out to him. "But it's yours," he protested.

"Take it," said Gabriel, quietly insistent. "My gift to you. Every boy needs a good watch, and I made this myself a long time ago. It may be a bit careworn, but I can vouch for the quality."

Not wanting to offend the angel, Jonathan held out his hand, and Gabriel placed the watch in his palm. "Thank you very much," he said.

Gabriel nodded, shook hands with Ignatius and Grimm, and left quietly.

"Well," said Ignatius. "That was something. I thought I knew that story, but I've never heard Gabriel tell it with so much detail, or so much passion."

Jonathan didn't know what to say — he just stared at the watch in his hand, running his thumb over the worn leather strap and the scuffed sapphire-glass face.

"Anyway, Grimm, where's that massive Pavlova you've been slaving over?" Ignatius added, hurriedly changing the subject.

Grimm brought out dessert, and they ate in near silence; even Elgar was quiet. There was something about the sadness of Gabriel's tale that made laughter seem inappropriate.

"Right," said Ignatius, once they had finished. "Hand me your dishes so Grimm and I can wash up."

After clearing the table, Cay thanked Grimm for cooking and said her goodbyes.

"I'll walk you back," said Jonathan. "I could do with some fresh air."

They left the vicarage and walked out into a chilly and moonlit night.

"Did Gabriel really not tell you that version of the story before?" he asked as they strolled across the green.

"No," said Cay. "He always left out the detail. Now I understand why he can be a bit distant sometimes — it's because he's sad." She looked up at the stars. "I wonder how long it takes you to fall from Heaven," she said.

Jonathan looked up too, wondering what it must be like to stand next to a star when it first exploded into life.

"Fancy a walk in the woods tomorrow?" asked Cay. "We can pack some sandwiches, and I can show you the lake."

"Cool," said Jonathan. "I'd like that."

They had reached Cay's house by then, and after saying good night Jonathan made his way back across the green. He turned to look at the dark forest and shivered; it felt like he was being watched. Hunching his shoulders, he hurried back to the warmth and light of the vicarage.

Chapter 10
CORVIDAE

Hidden in the dark of the forest, his pinstriped suit blending into the shadows, Rook watched as Jonathan scurried across the green and disappeared through the vicarage gates.

"Well, well," he murmured to himself, idly gouging chunks of bark from a nearby oak tree with his long, talon-tipped fingers. "If that's not the boy we've been looking for, I'll eat my hat." A red line appeared across the bottom half of the demon's face and split apart like an opening wound. His long, mottled tongue, forked at the tip, tasted the air like a snake.

Ceasing his surveillance, he turned and strode off to find his siblings. Pulling a silk handkerchief from his breast pocket, he dabbed at the sweat that trickled down his featureless face.

"I can see you," he said, mocking Hobbes End as he strode along. "But you can't see me, can you? It looks like Belial was right; we finally have a way in without being burned to a crisp!"

Raven was sitting in the driver's seat of the black Rolls-Royce, staring out the windscreen. Flowing from beneath the brim of her bowler hat, her long dark hair swept past the shoulders of her pinstriped suit. There was much to do, and Rook was late.

A snapping of twigs heralded the arrival of Crow, shambling toward Raven from the direction of the forest. In one clawed hand he held the mangled carcass of a freshly butchered pheasant. In his wake, a trail of feathers led back into the trees. Across Crow's face, a vivid smear of blood shone stark against his pale skin. Dropping his snack, he used the sleeve of his jacket to wipe away the gore. Opening the car door, he took off his bowler hat and got in next to Raven.

"Hungry," he said, looking at his sister for approval.

Raven nodded.

Content that he hadn't done anything wrong, Crow fixed his attention on the hat resting on his knees. He hummed tunelessly to himself while gently stroking the velvet nap of the brim. What Crow lacked in intelligence, he made up for in vicious, simple-minded brutality, and Raven liked her younger brother, very much.

There was a sharp rap on the driver's window. She lowered the glass to reveal the looming shape of Rook.

"The angel was telling the truth," he growled. "The boy's here. It looks like he's staying at the vicarage rather than with his grandfather, which seems odd to me. Time to report in."

Raven started the engine, and within minutes they were hurtling down deserted country lanes far from Hobbes End. Eventually they reached a pair of electronic security gates set into a towering yew hedge. The gates swung open, and Raven drove the Rolls-Royce up a long tree-lined drive, coming to a stop outside a large, fortified manor house.

Rook led his siblings through a cavernous entrance hall and up a wide oak staircase. He reached a leather-embossed door just off the landing and struck it with a clenched fist.

A moment of silence passed before a voice called out, "Enter."

Rook, Raven, and Crow—the three demons of the Corvidae—filed into the room. Before them, leaning against a huge mahogany writing desk, was Belial.

"Well?" asked the archdemon, his voice rasping through thin, cruel lips.

"Darriel's information proved correct," said Rook. "Jonathan's mother ran straight to Gabriel. She thinks he's safe in Hobbes End."

"Of course she does," said Belial. "After all, nothing evil can enter Hobbes End, can it? Gabriel made sure of that. Unless, of course . . ." Belial turned to look at the small wooden box sitting on his desk. "Unless, of course, you have some help. How did the field test go?"

"The village could sense I was there, but it couldn't see me," said Rook. "It must be quite frustrated."

"How much do we have left?" asked Raven.

"Enough to get hold of that boy," replied Belial. "I suggest you pay Hobbes End another visit tomorrow and persuade Jonathan that he'd be better off with me. I suspect you'll have to be firm with him — his father put up quite a fight, after all."

Crow gave vent to a laugh that sounded like a drain being unblocked.

"Did you leave Darriel where I told you?" asked Belial.

Raven nodded. "Right on the steps of Heaven itself."

"Still alive, I hope?"

"Barely."

"Good. I want him to be an example of what's coming

to anyone who stands in my way. And what of Jonathan's mother? What of the lovely, wayward Savantha?"

"We couldn't find her," said Raven. "She went back to the house, but we just missed her. We tracked her to the nearest Hell-gate but she'd already gone through."

"Where did the gate lead?" asked Belial.

"To Baal's domain."

Belial scowled. "She's probably heading to Lucifer to beg for his help. That might be a problem in the long run, but first she has to get past Baal. If he catches her, she'll wish she'd just cut her own throat. Well, she's a loose end that can wait for now—it's Jonathan I want. With the boy tamed and with his powers under my control, I'll be able to crush Baal and Lilith. Once I have their resources, I'll place my boot on Lucifer's neck and wipe that smirk off his arrogant face."

"And then?" asked Rook.

"And then this planet and everyone on it will be mine too. Humans have forgotten us, my bowler-hatted generals, but I will make them remember. With fire, sword, and blood I will show them what Hell on earth looks like!"

"And if Heaven decides to try to stop us?" asked Raven.

"I can't see that insane archangel doing anything but cowering behind his locked doors," said Belial. "No,

Raphael will be hiding in the dark until I see the opportunity to crush him. The gates of Heaven will open one day. When they do, I'll be waiting to finish the job that Lucifer was too weak to complete. He'll regret surrendering to Sammael — every second of the eternity it takes him to die."

"And what if Jonathan turns out to have no powers at all?" asked Raven. "What if he's just a freak of nature? What if we've spent the last twelve years chasing a ghost?"

Belial shrugged his shoulders. "Then you can eat him," he said. "And I have to go back to the drawing board. No point in wasting time on a lost cause."

The Corvidae grinned like sharks.

Chapter 11

A WALK IN THE WOODS

Jonathan woke to find the morning sun filtering through his bedroom curtains. Gently folding back the duvet, he swung his legs out of bed and walked over to the window, then opened the curtains and looked out over the village. It was so peaceful; a faint mist hugged the ground, and over by the green he could see the pond glittering in the sunlight. The gargoyles were having a heated discussion about something, and Grimm was returning from the village shop, morning paper under his arm and a bottle of milk in his hand.

Turning away, Jonathan noticed the watch that Gabriel had given him sitting on his bedside table. He walked over and picked it up. It was plain and simple, with a brown leather strap, a steel body, and black roman numerals on a white face. But it felt comfortable in his hand. On impulse, Jonathan turned the watch over and saw that the back plate bore an inscription. It read DEUS EX MACHINA.

It looks like Latin, he thought as he fixed the watch to his wrist. *I wonder what it means.* Promising himself that he'd ask Gabriel the next time he saw him, he showered, dressed, and ran down the stairs two at a time. He burst into the kitchen to find Grimm sitting at the table and munching on a huge slice of toast.

"Mumfffning, Junffun," mumbled Grimm, spraying crumbs everywhere.

"Morning," said Jonathan.

Sitting down next to Grimm, he buttered some toast and poured himself a mug of tea from the pot on the table. Taking a swig, he found his tongue assaulted by an awful mix of asphalt, sardines, and overcooked broccoli. He stuffed toast into his mouth, hoping it would take the taste away.

"I think I'll stick to orange juice," he said, getting up and looking in the fridge.

"Didn't you like the tea?" asked Grimm. "It's one I found right at the back of the pantry."

"Uh . . . no," Jonathan replied. "It tastes like I've been licking the road!"

"Hmm." Grimm frowned. "I thought it was just me. It really does taste awful, doesn't it?"

Jonathan nodded.

"Oh, well," said Grimm, tipping the contents of the teapot down the sink, "I won't be trying that one again. Come to think of it, it's been hidden at the back there for a very long time."

"What did it say on the tin?" asked Jonathan, his stomach turning over.

"Nothing," said Grimm. "It had a nice picture of some people at a party, watching boats on a river. Here, take a look." He picked up a square metal tin from the sideboard and handed it to Jonathan. It did indeed have a picture of people holding a party by a river. The men were wearing straw hats, and the women were dressed in smart period costume. Looking at the base of the tin, Jonathan found a tiny printed label that said LUNCHEON OF THE BOATING PARTY, 1881: PIERRE AUGUSTE RENOIR.

Jonathan shrugged. "It looks like an old biscuit tin to me. Oh, I'm going out for a walk with Cay today — have you got anything I can use for a packed lunch?"

"Well, there's some leftover omelet in the fridge, and there's my army water bottle and rucksack if you need it."

More egg, thought Jonathan, his stomach doing a queasy flip. "I think I'll get some sandwiches over at

Cay's house, if that's okay. But the rucksack and water bottle would be really handy."

"No problem," said Grimm, patting his stomach and belching loudly. He smacked his lips. "Oh, that tea really is repeating on me!"

Jonathan nodded and bent over to lace up his boots. He was just finishing when Elgar pushed his head through the cat flap. Seeing that Grimm wasn't lying in wait with his meat cleaver, Elgar squeezed himself through and jumped onto a chair. He had several small feathers stuck in his ears.

"Oi, cat!" rumbled Grimm as he rinsed out the teapot. "No nibbling on the toast."

"I wouldn't dream of it, old boy," snorted Elgar. "I've already had breakfast," he added, giving Jonathan a feral grin.

The thought of Elgar munching on some poor bird made Jonathan feel even more ill.

"Oh, you got out Renoir, I see," Elgar noted, examining the tin sitting on the table.

"Yep," said Grimm. *Luncheon of the Boating Party, 1881.*"

"Yes, I know what the painting's called," said Elgar, rolling his eyes. "I'm referring to the contents of the tin."

"Eh?" said Grimm, looking confused.

"Oh dear," muttered Elgar, jumping down and disappearing back through the cat flap. "Ask Ignatius . . ." were his last words.

A few moments of head scratching followed until Ignatius wandered into the kitchen in his bathrobe.

"Oh, where did you find this?" he asked, picking up the tin.

"In the pantry behind all the other tea," said Grimm, the fact that he may have made a serious error rapidly dawning on him.

"Tch, my memory!" Ignatius smiled. "Elgar did remind me I needed to send this to my mother. She forgot to take it when she moved to Devon."

"Sorry?" said Jonathan, a feeling of panic rising inside him along with his breakfast toast.

"Renoir's ashes," said Ignatius. "I'll pop them in the post later."

With a cheerful whistle the vicar wandered out the back door and into the garden to catch the morning sun. Standing on the patio, Elgar wandered over and sat next to him.

"Grimm made tea out of a dead dog's ashes, didn't he?" said the cat.

"Yep," said Ignatius.

From behind them came the sound of two people being noisily sick in the kitchen sink.

Amid a flurry of profuse apologies from Grimm and a barrage of smirking from Elgar, Jonathan finally left the vicarage. With his stomach still roiling after its unfortunate meeting with Renoir's ashes, he took deep breaths of cool morning air as he strode across the green to meet Cay.

He was dressed in jeans, walking boots, and a fleece, and slung over his shoulder was an old rucksack. Inside was a water bottle, a blanket, and a couple of apples.

As he walked, Jonathan waved good morning to the villagers who were up and about — Mr. Peters, who was sitting on his usual bench reading a book, and Mr. and Mrs. Flynn, who were taking a morning stroll.

Walking into the shop, he was greeted by Cay's head popping up from behind the counter.

"Morning," she said breezily. "Ready for a walk?"

"Yep," said Jonathan. "As long as we can make some sandwiches. I really couldn't face any cold omelet."

"Already sorted," said Cay. "You all right? You look a bit green."

"Don't ask," he replied.

They made their way along the hall and into the kitchen; sitting on the oak table were two piles of sandwiches.

"I've borrowed Grimm's water bottle," said Jonathan, retrieving it from inside the rucksack.

"You'd better give it a clean," suggested Cay. "It looks like it's not been used in a while."

"Good idea." Jonathan popped the cap off and shook it out over the sink. He was rewarded with a cloud of dust and two dead spiders. He gave the bottle a thorough rinse before filling it with fresh water. "Where's your dad today?" he asked.

"He's gone for his morning run," said Cay. "We may see him when we're walking." She looked out the window and smiled. "He loves the forest."

Putting the lid back on the bottle, Jonathan popped it into the rucksack along with the sandwiches. "Right," he said. "Let's go." He followed Cay through the back door and into the garden. Mrs. Forrester was kneeling on the grass nearby, tying some pea plants to a pyramid of bamboo canes. She smiled and waved as they walked past.

Leaving the garden behind, they followed a narrow path through the meadow and into the forest. It was a glorious morning, and despite his unpleasant breakfast, Jonathan found he was in a really good mood. He and Cay had bright sunshine, a cool breeze, and plenty of sandwiches. Perfect!

"I've been thinking about Gabriel," said Cay as they

struggled up a steep rise. "He seemed so sad when he finished telling his story. Should we go and see him later? Make sure he's okay?"

"I still can't believe he's actually an angel," said Jonathan. "We're living in the same village as an angel! And after all that's happened to him, he just wants to be ordinary. To get on with his life in peace."

"I know what you mean. I guess I've just never known anything different."

"Anyway, yeah," said Jonathan, struggling for breath. "Let's go and see him, as long as you don't mention your birthday present again!"

"I won't," said a grinning Cay. "Hey, can we stop for a minute? I could do with a rest."

Jonathan nodded. Leaving the path, they sat down on the mossy remains of a fallen tree.

"How did your dad end up as a werewolf?" he asked, handing Cay the water bottle.

She took a drink and paused. "Well, Mom and Dad don't like talking about it; they keep saying it's not important. Anyway, Dad was just born that way. His parents used to keep him locked up like an animal because they were scared of him. When he got old enough, he escaped and went traveling across Europe; that's when he met Mom, who was teaching at a school in Austria. His being a werewolf doesn't bother her, any more than

Gabriel's Clock

her being deaf bothers him. He can change shape whenever he wants to, and when he's a wolf he's not savage or
anything; he's just my dad in a wolf's body—except he
has a better sense of smell!"

"How did they end up here?"

"The same way everybody else does—they just arrived out of the blue. It's like the village calls to people."

A thought suddenly occurred to Jonathan. "Do you
think you'll take after your dad, given that you're half
werewolf?"

"Dunno." Cay shrugged. "No point worrying about
it. I haven't developed the urge to pee up trees yet!"

Jonathan laughed. "I'm surprised Elgar hasn't teased
you about it."

"Oh, he has," said Cay. "He said that at a full moon
I'll turn into an annoying, pint-size wolf with hearing
problems. I told him that if he ever said that again, I'd
mention it to Dad and that Elgar would end up as a
morning snack."

"Do werewolves eat cats?" asked Jonathan.

"I doubt it," said Cay. "And certainly not my dad.
But Elgar doesn't know that for sure." She grinned and
bounced her eyebrows up and down.

"Were you born here, then?" asked Jonathan.

Cay shook her head. "No, I was about two or three
when we arrived, but I can't remember living anywhere

else. Hobbes End has always been my home, although it can get a bit lonely at times. I'm scared of asking someone from school to come round to visit in case they see something that freaks them out."

"Yeah, that would be awkward," said Jonathan, remembering his own first reaction to the gargoyles and Elgar. "So, does anyone outside Hobbes End know what the village is? Do they know an angel crash-landed here?"

Cay shook her head. "No, I don't think so. People know the village exists, the postman delivers letters, and a man comes to read the gas meter, but it's like they don't see the real Hobbes End. Only people who live here do. It's funny, but the village knows who should be here and who's just visiting, and after a while it gently nudges visitors toward the exit."

Jonathan nodded. "It kept me here," he said, remembering. "I wasn't well enough to leave when I tried, so it stopped me. Anyway, what's your school like?"

"It's good, I enjoy it. I cycle there 'cause it's only five miles away. I go round to visit my friends' houses sometimes, but I guess they think I'm a bit weird for never asking anyone back here. They must think I'm either a snob or a slob!"

"Nah!" said Jonathan.

"I don't know what they think, really," said Cay. "I'm

just the girl from that little village in the forest, and sometimes I think people would be amazed to learn that we have electricity, running water, and everything!" She chuckled to herself. "It can be boring during the holidays, though. There's only so much you can do on your own." She looked at Jonathan and smiled. "That's why I'm glad you're here, strange boy. There hasn't been anyone my age in the village for a long time."

They both fell quiet as they ate one of the sandwiches Mrs. Forrester had made for them.

"Where did you go to school?" asked Cay.

"I've never been," said Jonathan, staring out over the forest. "We moved house all the time because of Dad's job, so Mom tutored me at home. I learned a lot, but it means that I know what it's like to be lonely too."

"It must have been exciting having a spy as a dad!"

"I don't know what he does, really; he would never say. I suppose if he is a spy, he wouldn't be able to tell me anyway. And then those . . . things came. I just see them as monsters, but I guess that's because I hit my head. I don't know who they were or why they attacked us either." He bit his lip and added sadly, "It's been over two weeks, and I still don't know where my parents are or why I'm here. I don't really know anything."

He hung his head. He liked being here in Hobbes End, he liked Cay and Elgar and Ignatius and Grimm;

he liked everyone. But every time he started to feel happy, he remembered that he had a list of questions as long as his arm, and nobody could give him any proper answers. He wondered if Gabriel could help him find his parents — he was an angel, after all . . .

Seeing that Jonathan was starting to brood, Cay resorted to throwing a handful of dead leaves at him. Jumping up, she shouted, "Last one to the lake carries the rucksack home!" and sprinted off into the trees.

By the time Jonathan got the leaf mulch out of his mouth and eyes, Cay had completely disappeared.

"Wait!" he cried out, getting to his feet and stuffing the water bottle into the rucksack. "I don't know which path goes to the lake . . . *Cay, wait!*"

Rapidly fading laughter was her only reply. With a groan of frustration he ran after her.

Rook watched from a distance as a disoriented Jonathan tore through the forest, his path taking him farther and farther away from the lake. Once he was sure that the boy was hopelessly lost, Rook melted into the trees, eager to finally introduce himself . . .

Chapter 12

An Unkindness of Raven

Cay burst out of the forest and onto the shore of the lake, her lungs burning as she panted for breath. Resting her hands on her knees, she tried to slow her thumping heart as little black spots danced before her eyes.

"Beat you, Jonathan. Beat you!"

Taking a deep breath, she stood up and looked about her. The lake was fringed by weeping willow trees, their branches trailing in the water, and Jonathan was nowhere to be seen. Cay suddenly wished she hadn't decided to race him here—apart from anything else, he had the water bottle and she was feeling very thirsty. Deciding to pass the time by walking farther round the lake, she pushed her way through curtain after curtain of willow, enjoying the sensation of being almost blind.

The branches parted to reveal a small clearing set back from the lakeshore, the still air filled with an extraordinary kaleidoscope of motion and color. Cay smiled, amazed at what she was seeing: butterflies — hundreds and hundreds of butterflies. Not wanting to disturb them, she inched forward to get a better look. To her delight, they didn't seem to mind her presence. One of them, its wings painted with copper and black, landed on her shoulder.

Suddenly every butterfly took to the air and fled the clearing. Cay shivered, a peculiar sensation rasping its way across her nerves, and she spun round, her heart in her mouth. But the clearing was empty.

"Hello?" she called out anyway. "Is anybody there?" There was no reply, just the faint sigh of the wind. Deciding to splash her face and neck with cool water, she headed back through the trees until she reached the edge of the lake. As the last branches parted, she found herself face to face with a nightmare.

Standing in front of her was a woman wearing a pinstriped suit and a bowler hat. The woman had long, dark hair — and no face!

Terror washed over Cay, and she let out the biggest

scream of her life. The woman's hand shot forward and closed around her throat like a vice, and Cay's eyes bulged, pain building in her chest as cruel fingers crushed her windpipe.

"Hello, child," came a chilling, sibilant voice. "I'm Raven of the Corvidae, and it's been too long since I last indulged myself. I've decided that while my brother has a chat with the boy, I might have some fun drowning you." Then the demon pushed Cay's head underwater and held it there.

"Great," said Jonathan. "I'm lost, Cay. *Thanks!*"

Standing in a forest clearing, he turned full circle and saw nothing but trees and bushes stretching off in all directions.

"Cay, where are you?" he shouted.

"A long way from here, boy," came a deep voice from behind him.

Jonathan swung round just in time to receive a harsh blow across his face. He sank to his knees and with watering eyes saw the blurry figure of a faceless man in a bowler hat. Panic filled him as he remembered where he had seen this thing before — in the cellar of the cottage just before his father had brought the ceiling crashing down.

"You're real!" Jonathan gasped.

"Oh, I'm very real, boy," the demon said to Jonathan, a mouth forming in the blankness beneath his hat—a red gash behind which jagged teeth could be seen gleaming. "Don't you recognize old Rook? The Corvidae have been hunting you for a very long time. Surely Mommy and Daddy must have warned you about us? Told you to run if you ever saw one of us?" Rook let out a gurgling chuckle.

"I don't know who you are. Why are you chasing me? Where are my parents?" Jonathan spat through clenched teeth. The world was spinning, and the only thing keeping him upright was the adrenaline of fear.

"Belial wants you, boy. He thinks you're going to end up leading his armies, a powerful, half-angel, half-demon general. Looking at you now, I can't really see it."

"Wh . . . what?" stammered Jonathan, the mention of the name Belial making his skin crawl just as it had at dinner the previous night. "Half angel, half demon? I'm human—what are you talking about?"

Rook tilted his head to one side in apparent puzzlement, then roared with laughter. "Oh, that's rich, that's positively delicious. Your parents didn't tell you what you are, did they? That is a cruel and unusual punishment, and I approve! You're going to be Belial's weapon to wield whether you like it or not, boy. You are far from human."

Jonathan scrambled backwards, a scream building in his throat. He collided with the trunk of a tree, and agony exploded outward from his still-healing skull fracture. He dimly heard a crack as the glass face of the watch Gabriel had given him broke.

"No point running," grinned Rook, baring those awful teeth, "or struggling, either. The outcome is inevitable, as your little girlfriend is finding out right about now."

Jonathan stared in horror. *Cay?* he thought. *They're after Cay, too?*

It was like a switch had been thrown inside him. An eerie calm descended, and all fear of the thing towering over him faded away. Rook was nothing; he was just a problem to be solved, an itch to be scratched. Then the anger came, and for a moment Jonathan thought he might explode as his vision went a weird shade of purple, and his shoulders screamed in agony as if the muscles of his back were laid bare. It was just like it had been when he'd faced Rook in the cellar.

"Kill him," said a voice in his head. "Rend him, tear him, gut him. He is not your equal."

Surging to his feet, Jonathan made a fist and punched the surprised Rook in the chest. As if he weighed nothing, the demon flew backwards across the clearing and slammed into a tree.

How did I do that? thought Jonathan as he watched Rook trying to regain his balance. The demon shook his head, black blood trickling from one of his ears and running down his neck as he faced Jonathan, then he drew back in what looked like fear. Jonathan blinked, his eyesight still blurry. It took him a moment to realize that Rook wasn't looking at him, but at something above and behind him. Jonathan slowly turned his head, staring at the towering mass of purple light that writhed in the air — light that grew from his shoulders!

With a crash Rook dived into the undergrowth and disappeared, leaving Jonathan alone in the clearing. He stood where he was, unsure of what was happening as the anger drained out of him. Something warm was running down his face, and he touched it with his fingertips and saw that they dripped crimson.

Far from human? he thought as he crumpled to the ground. Then everything went very, very black.

Ignatius stood in a quiet corner of the churchyard, not far from Gabriel's cottage. Next to him a rectangle of iron railings fenced in a horizontal slab of white marble. On the slab was a carved inscription:

ANGELA AND DAVID

BELOVED WIFE AND SON

ALWAYS IN MY HEART

Ignatius sighed. He had just turned to walk away when suddenly he doubled up in pain. He couldn't breathe; something was crushing his throat, and all he could see was dark water—he could even feel the coldness of it on his skin. He forced himself upright and with horror realized that Hobbes End was screaming at him inside his head, sharing the pain of someone who was in trouble, begging him to do something, and quickly.

There was a crash from Gabriel's cottage as the angel almost fell out of his front door, his face white. Clutching his chest, Gabriel met Ignatius's gaze.

"Something's hurting one of the children," the angel gasped. "The village is under attack."

"But where . . . ?" said Ignatius. "Oh my God, they're at the lake. They went for a walk to the lake." Cold panic seized him. "It's too far; we'll never get there in time."

"No—we won't," urged Gabriel. "But the gargoyles can!"

Ignatius ran faster than he ever had in his life. He tore back toward the vicarage, screaming out for Grimm and

Elgar at the top of his lungs. They met him at the gates, eyes wide and wondering what the hell was going on.

"Someone's trying to drown one of the children up at the lake," he gasped. "I don't know which one. Get up there as fast as you can—I'm going to send help!"

Without a second thought, Grimm and Elgar sprinted off toward the forest. Behind them, Ignatius turned to the gargoyles.

"Montgomery, Stubbs, you're free to leave your posts. Get to the lake, save the children. Do whatever you have to do."

"Fancy a quick spin up to the lake, Mr. Stubbs?" asked Montgomery.

"Indeed I do, Mr. Montgomery. Indeed I do," replied Stubbs.

Cackling with glee, the two gargoyles launched themselves skyward, across the village, and out over the forest.

"Crikey!" said Elgar as he ran into the forest beside Grimm. "I didn't know Monty and Stubbs could do that."

"They haven't been let off the leash for quite a while," Grimm said, panting, as he tore along. "So I think this is a good time to use 'em!"

The thundering in Cay's ears grew louder, and when she opened her eyes, they filled with water and she could see nothing but black. She began to thrash her body about, clawing at the hands wrapped around her throat. Nothing helped. Her lungs burned, and she opened her mouth to scream, but all that came forth was a small stream of bubbles. In the roaring of her oxygen-starved brain, Cay realized that she was about to die.

Suddenly the world spun as she felt herself picked up and thrown out onto land with jarring force. She coughed up water, then drew a ragged, painful — but very welcome — breath. Lying on the sodden ground and desperately trying to come to her senses, the sounds of a titanic struggle washed over her. Her vision swam as she struggled to raise her head, blinking to clear her sight. Two figures were fighting in the lake in front of her, slamming into each other again and again, bellowing and hissing.

As her eyes regained their focus she saw the pinstripe-suited monster that had been trying to drown her. The bowler hat had been knocked off her head, leaving a blank face framed by twisted ropes of wet hair. Crouching spiderlike in the churning lake, her attacker hissed through a mouth that was still nothing more than a crimson gash.

Then Cay gasped as she saw what had saved her.

Standing between her and her attacker stood a huge, misshapen male wolf, its silver-gray fur running with water and blood. The wolf's muzzle gaped to reveal a set of razor-edged fangs, and from sockets deep in its skull two yellow eyes blazed with defiance. Taking a breath deep into its barrel chest, it roared in fury.

"Dad?" croaked Cay.

The wolf turned to look at her, and for a second his gaze softened. This gave Raven the opening she'd been waiting for and she launched herself at the wolf, talons outstretched. He swung back but was too slow to stop her from gripping his right foreleg and wrenching it sideways. There was a sickening crack, and the wolf bellowed in pain. Enraged, he slammed his open mouth onto Raven's shoulder and bit down, hard.

This time it was Raven's turn to scream. With a powerful swing of his head the wolf sent the demon flying, then he began limping toward Cay. He hadn't gone more than a few feet when the seemingly unstoppable Raven launched herself out of the water. She landed on the wolf's shoulders, black demon blood pouring from the awful wound on her shoulder.

The wolf thrashed his head, trying to dislodge the demon while shielding his eyes. As he did so Raven lashed out at his damaged foreleg, driving him to his knees in pain.

With mounting horror, Cay saw that the broken leg was stopping her dad from rolling over and throwing off Raven. The monster was going to tear him to pieces and laugh while she did it.

Cay reached out with her hand and tried to scream, but her throat was too bruised to allow her more than a hoarse moan.

For one brief moment her dad returned her gaze. Then Raven cruelly jerked his head upward, her talons ready to tear out his throat.

And then the cavalry arrived.

"Incoming!" hooted Montgomery and Stubbs in perfect unison, slamming into Raven with the force of two well-thrown granite bowling balls.

Raven didn't have time to react. She was torn from the wolf's back and flung out over the lake, flailing and tumbling before hitting the water with incredible force. Stubbs, positively volcanic with rage, clung onto Raven's hair with one hand and punched her as hard as he could with the other, hammering the demon almost senseless. Montgomery was about to join in when the wolf collapsed into the lake, the water closing over his head.

"Dad!" Cay cried, crawling as fast as she could toward her wounded father.

"Duty calls," shouted Montgomery, pulling his

friend off the struggling Raven. "We've got to help Mr. F."

"Right," said Stubbs, giving Raven one last punch right between where her eyes should have been. Streaking off after Montgomery, he left the battered demon barely conscious in the water.

With the assistance of the gargoyles, a sick and dizzy Cay managed to pull her father to safety. Sitting by his side, Cay gently stroked the wolf's torn and matted fur and watched the rise and fall of his chest, averting her eyes from his shattered front leg. Montgomery stood next to her, resting his granite paw on her shoulder. Stubbs sat by the wolf's head, patting it reassuringly.

An awful thought crawled its way into Cay's shocked mind. "Jonathan!" she gasped. "Oh God, what if there are more of those things? What if he's being attacked too?"

"We can go find him?" suggested Montgomery.

"Oh please, Monty," said Cay. "We'll be all right now. It's my fault he got lost. Please let him be okay."

"No need to panic," said Stubbs. "We'll sort it. C'mon, Mr. Montgomery." Like pebbles from a slingshot, the two gargoyles arced skyward and away over the trees.

It seemed like an age, but the change Cay had seen

so many times finally began. Fur withdrew and was replaced by skin. Muscle and bone changed shape, melted, flowed into one another, as the wolf's body redesigned itself. Through her tears, she saw the wonderfully familiar, heavily bearded face of her father. He looked back at her through eyes that were tight with pain, but still he smiled. His right arm was badly broken just below the elbow, jagged bones protruding through the skin.

Cay laid her head against her father's chest and wept. "Thanks, Dad," she whispered.

Kenneth Forrester kissed her forehead, holding her tightly with his one good arm. He glanced warily at the lake. There was no sign of his adversary, just a battered bowler hat floating on the surface of the water.

And at that moment Grimm and Elgar came crashing through the trees. "It's okay," said Kenneth. "The boys got here in time."

"Only just, from the looks of it," said Grimm, shocked at what he saw. Taking off his jacket, he gently wrapped it round Kenneth to keep him warm.

"I know the arm looks nasty, but it'll mend quickly once you set the bones. One of the benefits of being a werewolf!"

Other voices called from nearby — voices filled with concern.

"Over here!" Grimm bellowed.

Within moments, Ignatius, Gabriel, and a frantic Joanne Forrester burst into the clearing. Mrs. Forrester's expression of anguish melted when she saw her family, and she rushed toward her husband and daughter, enfolding them gently in her arms. Grimm smiled at her and, after tearing a strip off his shirt, set to work on Kenneth's broken arm.

"Where's Jonathan?" asked Elgar.

A shiver ran down Ignatius's spine as he realized that the boy wasn't there.

"We got separated," said Cay from deep within her mother's embrace. "I was racing him here and he didn't arrive. He must be lost. Monty and Stubbs have gone to look for him. I'm sorry . . ." Tears ran down her cheeks.

"It's all right, Cay," said Ignatius. He turned and took Gabriel aside. "Is the village telling you anything?"

Gabriel shook his head. He was trying to look calm, but the fear in his eyes betrayed him. "Mercifully the village isn't worried about Jonathan. Cay's right, though — he's in the forest somewhere, not too far away."

"I'm getting the same thing," said Ignatius. "The gargoyles will find him, don't worry."

"But I am worried," said Gabriel. "What just happened to Cay and her father doesn't make sense."

"Would you keep watch for Monty and Stubbs while I find out the details?" said Ignatius. "Then we'll know what to do." Gabriel nodded, and Ignatius walked back to where Cay sat with her father and kneeled down next to them. "What attacked you, Kenneth? It must have been strong to hurt you in your wolf form."

"It was female, I think. Human size and shape but with talons at the ends of her fingers. Strong and very fast. She looked odd, though — she wore a business suit and a bowler hat!"

"And she didn't have a face," said Cay. "Just before she grabbed me, she said something. She said that her name was Raven and that she was of the Cor-something. I can't really remember . . ."

Ignatius felt his stomach drop like a stone. He turned to look at Gabriel and saw that the angel's face was as white as a sheet. The Corvidae had somehow managed to get into Hobbes End! There was only one reason that they would suddenly appear like this — and that reason was Jonathan.

"Do you know what it was?" asked Kenneth, wincing as Grimm reset his arm.

"Yes," said Ignatius. "Something terrible that should not be able to come anywhere near the village. I'm so sorry you were hurt."

"We're both alive," said Kenneth. "And that's good enough for me. I've never been so pleased to be a were-wolf! I was out on my run and smelled something strange, something I didn't like. I could tell the trail was heading toward the lake, and knowing that's where the kids were, I ran flat out to get here."

Ignatius smiled and nodded. And then there was a whistling sound and a thump as Montgomery plummeted from the sky.

"We found Jonathan," he said. "He's in a clearing about twenty minutes' walk away. He's had another bang to the head, but he's okay. Mr. Stubbs stayed with him for safety."

"Thank God," said Ignatius. "Gabriel and I will go get him. Grimm, you take everyone else home and put the kettle on. We need to sit down and figure out what to do next. If the Corvidae can somehow enter Hobbes End, then we have a very big problem."

"What do you mean?" asked Grimm.

"It means my worst fears have come true," said Gabriel, lowering his voice so only Ignatius and Grimm could hear. "Not only can the Corvidae get past our defenses, but Belial now knows where Jonathan is. Now we have an archdemon who might be able to walk straight in and just take Jonathan from us!"

Ignatius paced up and down the patio behind the vicarage. Clutched in his hand was a large and tepid mug of Renoir-free tea.

"Stop it. You're driving me nuts," said Elgar, poking his head out from beneath the garden seat.

"Sorry," apologized Ignatius. "But I'm really worried about Jonathan. He didn't say much on the way home, just that he'd been attacked by the same thing that came for him at his family's cottage and that it called itself Rook."

"So was it the Corvidae that attacked them?" asked Elgar. "I wondered what you and Gabriel were whispering about after Monty came back. Last week when he was laid up, he was telling Cay and me about these things. He thought he'd imagined them because of the knock on his head. But he didn't, did he? It was them. Is that why he's here? Is he hiding? Hang on — if the Corvidae are after him, then that means . . ." Elgar's eyes went wide. "It means that a certain archdemon is after Jonathan too! Why didn't you tell me?"

Ignatius nodded and sighed. "Look, Elgar, there's a lot I haven't told you, but up until now we've been trying to keep Jonathan's location secret. I'm good at keeping secrets, remember? Have I told anyone about your history with Belial and the Corvidae?"

"Good point," said Elgar. "I'll just have to restrain my curiosity."

"I'll give you the whole story once I've talked to

Jonathan, I promise," said Ignatius. "I just need to figure out what to do next." He looked through the kitchen window and saw that Gabriel and Grimm had come downstairs. "If you'll excuse me, Elgar."

The cat shrugged and remained in the garden while Ignatius went inside.

"How is Jonathan?" he asked Grimm.

Grimm's lips were set in a thin line. "The scar on the back of his head has opened up again, and there are these huge bruises on his back and shoulders. I am not — I repeat, *not* — happy!"

"Neither am I, Halcyon," said Ignatius.

Gabriel sighed. "Those bruises . . . it's all happening too soon."

"What is?" asked Ignatius.

"The power that's inside him is what caused those bruises. I hoped he'd say something to us on the way home, tell us exactly what happened, but he's so scared."

"Why would the power inside him cause those bruises?" asked Grimm.

"It's his wings," said Gabriel. "I'm sure of it. He felt threatened by Rook, so they just tore themselves out from his shoulders without being summoned. That's not supposed to happen — he should manifest them gently — but he doesn't know how to, doesn't even know what he is! I hoped that I would have the time to teach him how to control them, but that takes years."

"He's going to have wings?" gasped Grimm.

Gabriel nodded. "Yes, he is, but I don't know what they'll look like. Angels develop wings with feathers, and demons tend to have wings similar to those of a bat. The only exceptions I know of are my siblings and I. Our wings are different—they're made from ribbons of intelligent, solid light, and they're incredibly powerful. They're like windows into the heart of creation itself."

"And Jonathan might have wings like yours?" asked Ignatius.

"Possibly," said Gabriel. "But I can't be sure. The blend of angel and demon inside him has opened a door to somewhere very powerful, and he has no idea how to control it. It's why the village wasn't worried about him; it knew Jonathan was strong enough to defend himself. But if Jonathan gets scared and manifests those wings too often, the shock could kill him."

"Dear God," said Ignatius. "What on earth are we going to do?"

"We damn well tell Jonathan what he is," said Grimm. "The poor lad's been through enough. We can't wait for his parents any longer; you have to tell Jonathan the truth."

"I agree," said Gabriel. "I'll do it first thing tomorrow, after he's had a good night's rest."

"And what about defending against the Corvidae in the meantime?" asked Ignatius. "Monty and Stubbs are going to be fast asleep for at least a couple of days while they recharge their batteries. It's why they're not allowed to fly except in an emergency."

Gabriel frowned and nodded. "I know, but there's nothing we can do about that now. As for the Corvidae, I think they'll lick their wounds for today, but they'll be back — and soon. They know where Jonathan is now, and they won't stop until they have him. The whole village is in danger while Jonathan is here, so he has to leave."

"What? You're just going to throw him out?" barked Grimm.

"No, Grimm, you misunderstand," said Gabriel, sorrow written across his face. "I would die before I let Belial have Jonathan as well as my son."

"Oh, Gabriel, I am so sorry," said Grimm. "Please forgive me."

"It's all right, Grimm. There is always hope, and I may have a way to save Jonathan. I just need time to figure out if it's possible. I'll speak to you in the morning, when hopefully I'll have the answer."

The old angel left the vicarage kitchen, looking as though he bore the weight of the world on his shoulders.

"What do we do now?" asked Grimm.

"Have a glass of single-malt whiskey," said Ignatius, "while I figure out how to tell everyone who lives in Hobbes End that Hell has come to their sanctuary."

Chapter 13
BRUISES

Hobbes End is under threat," said Ignatius, his fingers gripping the edge of the pulpit. "For the first time since Gabriel landed here, evil has come to our home. This is something I will not—cannot—tolerate!" He banged his fist on the lectern to emphasize how angry he was.

"Hear, hear!" came a voice from the back of the church.

Ignatius looked out over the congregation and smiled. "Thank you."

"Nae problem," replied Angus McFadden, a longtime resident who lived next door to Cay. "Something that hurts a wee child is gonnae get a slap if I get my hands on it. Ye ken?"

Appreciative murmurs rang around the packed church, and Ignatius felt glad to be in the company of such people. Everyone in the village was here, except for Grimm and Elgar, who were watching over Jonathan; Mr. and Mrs. Forrester, who were sitting with Cay; and Gabriel, who was working in his cottage.

First thing that morning Ignatius had asked the whole village to assemble in the church. He wanted to explain that somehow the impossible had happened, that evil had managed to get past the village defenses. He'd hoped that the inhabitants of Hobbes End wouldn't panic, but Ignatius was astonished by the strength of their response.

"This is our home!" cried Lucia Silkwood, her prized aspidistra sitting next to her on a pew at the front of the church. "Tell us what we can do to defend it. I'm not scared of some bogeymen, and neither is Henry."

"Henry?" asked Ignatius.

"Henry," said Lucia, gesturing to the plant next to her.

"Of course," said Ignatius, nodding politely at the aspidistra.

"Why are these things, these Corvidae, here?" asked Clara and Cecily Hayward. "They're not after our owls, are they?"

"No," said Ignatius. "These monsters are not after

any of you. They're after our new arrival. They're after Jonathan."

A gasp went up, and Ignatius looked out over a sea of shocked faces. "They came for Jonathan yesterday, but he fought one of them off. They hurt Cay simply because they could, because they enjoy it."

"But why are they chasing Jonathan?" asked Mr. Flynn, sitting next to his wife and holding her hand protectively. "He's such a nice lad."

"Yes, he is," said Ignatius. "But he has power that an archdemon wants to use."

"Damned if we'll let that happen!" shouted Professor Morgenstern. "I've got hand grenades, you know. Built them myself."

Ignatius blinked and made a mental note to see the professor about that later.

"Jonathan may be in danger," said Mr. Peters, getting to his feet. "But he's not alone. This is Hobbes End, and we look out for each other!"

Like a wave, everyone stood up to join Mr. Peters, shouting their defiance at the creatures that dared to invade their home.

Ignatius, momentarily overcome by their support, looked at a stone plaque on the church wall to his right. The name on it said SALVADOR CRUMB.

"You watching this, Dad?" said Ignatius with a smile.

There was some shushing, and everyone except Mr. Peters sat down. "Tell us what to do," he said. "How can we help?"

"I want you all to go home and stay vigilant," said Ignatius. "These things are vicious, and I don't want any of you getting hurt. Gabriel, Grimm, and I will fight these things if they reappear, so if you see anything, call the vicarage immediately. We have a plan to keep Jonathan safe, but until we set it in motion I want you all inside and out of harm's way. What say you?"

The roar of agreement almost lifted the roof off the ancient church.

Jonathan awoke, struggling through layers of cotton wool that filled his head. His mouth felt like it had squirrels living in it, and the astringent tang of witch hazel stung the inside of his nose. Elgar was sitting on the windowsill and peering through the glass, his breath making little fog patches.

"What time is it?" asked Jonathan.

"Half past nine," said Elgar. "You've just missed a big village meeting. I can see everyone rushing home, so I guess Ignatius told them all about what happened yesterday." The cat jumped down from the sill and came to sit on the bed. "How're you feeling? As my mother would say, you look like you've been in the wars."

"I feel like I ran into a tree," said Jonathan. "Which isn't far from the truth."

"You've got yet more nasty bumps on your head," said Elgar. He paused a moment. "You're lucky to be alive, you know. Very few people have fought one of the Corvidae and lived."

Jonathan went quiet. "Is that what those things are called?"

Elgar nodded.

"Do you know something about them?"

"A little bit," said the cat, but he seemed reluctant to say more. "The one who attacked you is called Rook," he added.

Jonathan paused. In his head he could still see the thing. "They're the ones who attacked my home — I'm sure of it. I wasn't making it up, you know, head injury or not."

"I believe you," said Elgar.

"I thought I was supposed to be safe here," sighed Jonathan. "I thought nothing evil could get into the village?"

"That's the theory," said Elgar. "The fact that those demons —"

"Demons?" asked Jonathan.

Elgar sighed. "Yes, they're demons. And really, really unpleasant ones. They're connected with the archdemon Belial. Do you remember Gabriel mentioning him at dinner the other night? He is seriously bad news. That the Corvidae can somehow enter Hobbes End is driving Ignatius and Gabriel nuts. What I can't figure out is why they're risking coming here at all."

Jonathan was only half listening to his friend; he knew why the Corvidae were in Hobbes End—they were looking for him because he was "far from human." And that terrified him.

"So how did you fight off Rook?" asked Elgar.

"I'm not sure," said Jonathan. "I just got really angry and knocked him across the clearing with a single punch."

Elgar blinked in astonishment. "Wow! Bet that surprised him."

"I don't think he was expecting it," said Jonathan. "But when he said that they were after Cay, too, I just wanted to kill him. There was this voice in the back of my head. It was telling me to . . . to tear him apart. And I really, really wanted to, but then there was this purple light and I . . ." Jonathan rubbed his face and sighed heavily. "Cay's all right, isn't she? Ignatius said she was."

"She'll have a sore throat for a bit," said Elgar. "But she's a tough little cookie. Annoying as Hell, but tough. I guess she has some werewolf blood in her after all."

Jonathan gave the cat a weak smile, but he couldn't

stop thinking about what Rook had said, and of the purple light that had grown from his shoulders.

"Why do I get the feeling you're not telling me everything?" said Elgar, twitching his whiskers.

Jonathan fell silent again and looked at his lap. Elgar, unusually patient, sat and peered at his friend with curious eyes. Then, "Rook said that I wasn't human," Jonathan blurted out. "He said that I was the only half-angel, half-demon child in existence and that Belial wants to use me as a weapon. He said that my parents had been lying to me!" Tears ran down his face, as much from confusion as from the thumping in his head caused by his injuries.

"Ah," said Elgar. "So that's it. I knew there was something going on. My whiskers never fail me. Added to which, you smell funny."

Jonathan wiped his eyes. "I smell funny?" He couldn't help a small grin.

"Yeah," said Elgar. "I have a very good nose, and you don't smell like anything I've ever come across. It's not that you whiff like the bottom of a dirty linen basket or anything, just that you smell different."

"Not human?"

Elgar shook his head. "Definitely not human."

"Oh," said Jonathan.

"Is it such a bad thing?" said Elgar. "Where's the fun

in being ordinary? Let's face it, who wouldn't want a talking cat for Christmas?" He butted Jonathan in the stomach with his head. "See? Made you smile."

Jonathan scratched Elgar behind the ears. "What do I do now?"

"Hmm," said the cat. "I'd go and find Gabriel and ask him to explain what's actually going on. You need to be careful, though — the Corvidae could pop up again at any moment. You'd better ask Grimm to be a body-guard. Don't go for a walk in the woods, eh?"

Cay sat up in bed, a bandage wrapped round her throat. She cradled a large mug of hot chocolate and tried to swallow, even though it really hurt.

"Are you sure you're all right?" her mother signed.

"Yeah," Cay croaked. "I just want to go and see if Jonathan's okay."

Her mother nodded, her fingers a blur. "Grimm did say that he was in one piece, just a bit shell-shocked. Now, you aren't going to start blaming yourself for what might have happened to him, are you?"

"No, Mom," she said. "I'm just worried about him, that's all. And Dad . . . how's his arm?"

Mrs. Forrester gave Cay's leg a squeeze. "That's my girl. I'll go and make you some breakfast. And don't worry about your dad—you know how quick he heals. His arm is almost as good as new already."

Cay smiled, but once her mother had left the room she climbed out of bed and walked to the window. Staring out into the drizzle, she saw the light from Jonathan's room. "How did you escape from that thing, Johnny?" she wondered aloud. "How did you escape?"

"Do you think Gabriel will mind me going to see him?" Jonathan asked Grimm as he walked to the church with Elgar trotting along beside them.

"I don't think he'll mind at all," said Grimm. "In fact, I think he'll probably have quite a lot to say."

Jonathan was about to ask Grimm what he meant by this when Cay came running down the road toward them and gave Jonathan a huge hug that almost knocked him off his feet.

"Hey, nice lump!" she whispered, pointing to the swelling behind his ear.

"Yeah, it's nasty, isn't it?"

"Mine's better, though," Cay added. She unwound her scarf to reveal a livid bruise circling her neck from ear to ear. Stark against the blue and green discoloration were finger marks.

"Oh, Cay!" Jonathan gasped, horrified at her injuries. "It's all my fault. If they hadn't been after me, you wouldn't have gotten hurt."

"Don't be daft," she said croakily. "It's not your fault. Anyway, how did you escape? I had this thing that called herself Raven trying to drown me. The only reason I'm still alive is that I had Dad, Monty, and Stubbs all giving her a good kicking. You didn't have anyone, and it's my fault you got lost. I forgot you didn't know the path to the lake." Her face was pale and sad.

Jonathan remained silent, staring at his feet.

"How did you get away?" Cay asked again.

Grimm put a huge, reassuring arm round Jonathan's shoulder.

"The thing that attacked me called itself Rook. I knocked him across a clearing and into a tree," whispered Jonathan.

"But those things are incredibly strong," said Cay, amazed. "Raven managed to break Dad's arm when he was in his wolf form. And I couldn't budge her fingers from round my throat!"

"Rook said they were after you, too, so I just got really angry and hit him."

"But that's brilliant!" said Cay. "Perhaps you're a superhero like in the films or something and you just don't know it!" She stopped talking when she saw how distressed Jonathan was. "What's the matter?" she asked him.

"Rook said something to me," replied Jonathan.

Cay held her breath.

"He said that I wasn't human. That I was half angel, half demon." He looked pleadingly at Cay. "What am I?" he asked. "*Who* am I?"

"That's what we're here to find out," said Grimm. "Now, you go and see Gabriel while I wait here and keep watch."

They made their way toward Gabriel's cottage, but as they passed the church they saw that the door was open. Someone was speaking inside.

"That sounds like Gabriel," said Cay.

Stepping quietly through the door, the smells of damp stone, furniture polish, and fresh flowers quickly surrounded them. They could see Gabriel sitting in a pew at the front of the church and talking to the stained-glass window above the altar. The window showed an angel dressed in black armor and clutching a long-bladed spear in his right hand. The blade rippled with white flame, and the angel looked off to one side as if searching for an enemy.

Gabriel turned his head to look at Jonathan and Cay as they stood near the door. "Come and sit with me," he said. "We need to talk."

They walked along the aisle and sat down next to him as requested. For a moment the old angel didn't say anything; he just kept looking at the window, his face sad.

"It's an image of my brother Michael," Gabriel said eventually. "He didn't look so fierce in real life. He laughed a lot, and I miss him. I often come and talk to him when I'm troubled." He sighed, and as he turned to face him Jonathan felt the same sensation of familiarity that he always felt when he was near the angel. Only this time it was much, much stronger.

"Why do I feel like I know you?" asked Jonathan.

Gabriel smiled, then frowned as he saw the damaged watch on Jonathan's wrist.

"I'm sorry I broke the glass," said Jonathan. "I knocked it against a tree when Rook hit me."

"It wasn't your fault," said Gabriel. "Here, give me the watch and I'll fix it for you today. It's the least I can do."

Jonathan undid the strap and handed the watch over. "Why did you give it to me?" he asked. "Books and cards and sweets I can understand, but this was your watch, and I'm just some kid."

"You're not just some kid," said Gabriel, giving Jonathan a sad smile. "You're my grandson."

"*What?*" gasped Cay. She nudged Jonathan excitedly. "See? I said you were a superhero or something."

Gabriel chuckled. "You're not a superhero, Jonathan; in fact, I'm not sure what you are, exactly. But I do know that you are family, and that you are precious to me beyond measure."

Jonathan's head swam. Everything he had thought was true was turning out to be a big fat lie.

"Who am I?" he asked. "And what about Mom and Dad . . . ?"

"Right," said Gabriel. "This is the short version. You'll have to wait until I've got you somewhere safer than here, then you can ask me all the questions you like. Okay?"

Jonathan nodded.

"Your parents *are* your parents, but they are not really called Daniel and Sarah Smith. Your father is my son, Darriel, and your mother is Savantha, a demon. You're a mixture of both, and the only one of your kind. Ever since your birth, Belial's been trying to find you. You hold an astonishing power inside you, Jonathan, and he wants it."

Jonathan sat with his mouth open. He was having trouble comprehending what Gabriel — his grandfather — was telling him. It was only the feeling of Cay reaching out and squeezing his hand in reassurance that kept him from spinning off into hysteria.

"I thought Dad worked for the government, something secret, and that's why we had to keep moving house and why I couldn't go to school and why . . ." He ran out of things to say. Despite that what Gabriel was telling him was incredible, deep down inside him it made some kind of sense.

"Your parents weren't moving for the sake of your father's career," said Gabriel. "They were moving to try to keep you safe. To try to keep one step ahead of Belial and the Corvidae."

"Could Belial really do what Rook said he could?" asked Jonathan. "Could he turn me into a weapon?"

"Yes, I think he could," said Gabriel. "Belial is ancient — very intelligent and evil beyond redemption. Do not underestimate him as I appear to have done. Your parents just wanted you to have a normal life, Jonathan. They were trying to protect you. Please don't hate them for that."

"I don't hate them — I just wish they'd told me!" cried Jonathan.

"I know." Gabriel sighed. "Everything always looks so clear in hindsight. I wanted you all to live here, where you were born, but if there's one thing angels are, it's stubborn — and my son is no exception."

"I was born here?" gasped Jonathan.

Gabriel smiled. "I have your crib in my cottage."

"Is that why this place feels so familiar, so like home?"

"Yes," said Gabriel. "You can leave Hobbes End, but it never leaves you."

"But what happened to Mom and Dad? Where are they?"

Gabriel swallowed hard and turned to face Michael's window once again. Jonathan could see the distress in the old angel's face. It mirrored what he was feeling inside.

"I don't know is the answer," said Gabriel. "Grimm went to check your old cottage soon after you first arrived. There was no sign of either of your parents. I'm hoping that your mother is making her way to Lucifer for help. It's a huge risk, and the journey will be difficult, but if she reaches him, she may at least gain a measure of protection."

"And Dad?"

Gabriel swallowed hard and closed his eyes. "Creation grant my son the strength to endure."

To Jonathan it sounded like a prayer. Then all the pieces fell together, leaving him with a picture that he didn't want to see. "They've got him, haven't they?" he stammered. "It's . . . it's how the Corvidae knew where to find me. Belial's got Dad and he's hurt him, hasn't he?" Tears spilled down his face. "Is Dad dead?"

Gabriel shook his head. "I don't think so. I would have felt his passing, and he wouldn't have revealed your location without a fight. Belial will not have been . . . gentle . . . with him, though."

Jonathan heard that voice inside him again, the one he'd heard during his fight with Rook, the one that urged him to destroy.

"I want to kill Belial," he said coldly. "I want to make him suffer for what he's done."

Gabriel sighed and placed a hand on Jonathan's shoulder. "It's speaking to you, isn't it?"

"What is?" asked Jonathan.

"You know what I mean," said Gabriel. "That voice inside you."

"Is it because I'm half demon?" Jonathan asked. "Do I have this evil side?"

Gabriel shook his head. "Life's not so black and white, my boy. Angels and demons are more alike than you would think. Your mom is just as good as your dad. What you're hearing is the voice of power. The more power you have, the louder it shouts. Humans have a saying, that power corrupts, and that absolute power corrupts absolutely, but they have no idea how true that is. You are powerful, Jonathan. I don't know how powerful yet, because there's never been anyone like you before. It's the reason Belial wants you, and it's the reason you always need to be on your guard against that voice. Never let it rule you."

"What happens if I can't control it?"

"Then you turn into another Lucifer, and you end up destroying that which you profess to love."

"Oh . . ." Jonathan sighed.

"Don't worry, grandson," said Gabriel. "I'll teach you all I can. Show you how to use those wings of yours without hurting anyone."

"Is that what scared Rook away? Those big purple things that grew out of my shoulders? Were they my wings?"

Gabriel nodded. "Once you know how to control them they manifest at your command. It looks like the mixing of angel and demon genes has somehow given you wings that are as powerful as mine once were, maybe even more so. The Corvidae will be wary of attacking you head-on after the scare you gave Rook."

"But my shoulders are all bruised," said Jonathan. "They really hurt."

"I know," said Gabriel. "It's because you haven't had time to learn what they are, what they can do, to manifest them gently. You just reacted instinctively to a threat when Rook attacked you. It's no wonder it hurt — all that power ripping its way out of you unchecked. Whatever happens, you must try to keep it under control, not let anger take over. Each time it happens it damages your body, and I don't know how much more you can take."

Jonathan's heart sank. "Will you help me? Teach me to control it?"

"Of course I will, Jonathan," said Gabriel. "But right now we have to get you away from Belial and the Corvidae or we'll never get the chance."

"How are they getting into Hobbes End?" asked Cay.

Gabriel shook his head. "I just don't know, Cay. I'm going to figure it out, but it'll take time, and that's a luxury we don't have. Jonathan, I've been thinking about this since you were attacked, and I need to hide you somewhere else. Somewhere Belial and the Corvidae can't possibly go."

"But where?"

"My old workshop in Heaven," said Gabriel.

"But didn't you say Heaven was all locked up?" asked Cay.

Gabriel nodded. "My brother Raphael may have locked the gates, but I think that with the right key I may be able to open a back door. If I work all day, I can have it finished by tonight. Then I can sneak Jonathan into Heaven without Raphael knowing. Once he's safe, I can figure out how to fight the Corvidae."

"That's genius!" said Cay.

"But how could you open a door into Heaven?" asked Jonathan.

"Given the complexity of what I'm trying to do," said Gabriel, "there's only one sort of key that will suffice."

"Like what?" asked Cay.

"What do you think?" said Gabriel. "It'll have to be a clock!"

Up above, crouching in the belfry and listening to every word that Gabriel said, Rook smiled.

"Would you like some fresh tea, Elgar?" asked Grimm, placing a bowl in front of the cat.

"There's no dog in it, is there?"

"No, there's no dog in it!" snapped Grimm. "What's left of Renoir is boxed up and ready to be sent to Devon. I suggest you never mention it again. If Ignatius's mom finds out what I did, we'll all be in for it."

"He's right," said Ignatius, from behind that day's paper.

"Discretion is indeed the better part of valor," said Elgar, dunking his face in the tea.

They heard voices in the vicarage hallway. Moments later Jonathan and Cay walked in, Jonathan looking worried. Cay, knowing how nervous he was, gave his hand a brief squeeze.

"We've got something to tell you," said Jonathan.

Elgar looked up from his bowl, tea dripping from his whiskers. "You're not getting married, are you?"

Muffled snorting came from around the table.

"No, we're not getting married, kipper brain!" protested Cay.

"It's all right," said Jonathan. "Can I have some tea?"

"Yep," said Grimm, reaching for the pot.

"There's no dog in it, is there?"

"*No. There's no flippin' dog in the tea!*" snarled Grimm.

"Don't worry about him," Elgar reassured Jonathan. "Did you find Gabriel?"

"Yeah, he told me everything. And he said you already know who I really am."

"We weren't hiding anything from you on purpose, Jonathan," said Ignatius. "We were just helping Gabriel try to keep you safe."

"I know, and that's why Gabriel asked me to come over and tell you his plan while he gets things ready."

"What plan is that, Jonathan?" asked Grimm.

"Gabriel's going to sneak me into Heaven by a secret back door that he built into his old workroom."

There was a plop as Ignatius's pipe fell out of his mouth and into his cup of tea. "I see," he said, a stunned look on his face. "Then I guess you'd better sit down and give us the details!"

Chapter 14

GABRIEL'S CLOCK

In the attic of his cottage, Gabriel sat slumped at his workbench. His hands shook, his breathing was labored; he was utterly exhausted. On the scarred wood in front of him lay the most difficult piece of engineering he'd ever attempted. It had taken most of the day and almost all the power he had left, but he didn't begrudge an ounce of it.

"I've done it," the angel said to himself, his voice hoarse. "You're going to be safe, Jonathan."

A shadow flickered above him, and Gabriel raised his weary head just in time to see the skylight in the roof explode inward. Shards of glass rained down as Rook, Raven, and Crow plummeted to the floor.

Without hesitation Gabriel grabbed with both hands

a glass sphere that sat on the bench in front of him. The sphere contained an incredibly complex clock mechanism, with the numerals for hours and minutes etched onto the inside of the glass. With a grunt of effort he threw the sphere at a door built into the gable wall, and the door flew open to reveal the impossible—a desert landscape stretching off into the distance as far as the eye could see. The sphere sailed through the doorway in a graceful arc to land with a thump in the soft sand beyond.

"Guard it, Brass!" croaked Gabriel.

Rook snarled and dived for the open doorway, just to have it slam shut in his face. He grabbed the handle and wrenched the door open again to reveal nothing but a brick wall.

Gabriel allowed himself a weary chuckle. "You'll never see Heaven, monster." He sighed.

Rook turned and snarled as Raven and Crow grabbed the weakened angel's arms.

With inhuman force, Rook dealt Gabriel a backhanded blow that knocked him across the room and into an oak bookcase. Gabriel slumped to the floor as his precious books cascaded around him. His vision began to dim, and he could just make out the figure of Rook standing above him.

"I may not see Heaven," hissed the demon, "but I'll make damn sure you get to see Hell."

Gabriel smiled through the pain as Rook rained blows upon him. "Deus ex machina," he whispered as consciousness slipped away.

In the vicarage kitchen Ignatius lowered the *Times* to reveal his ashen face. He stood up, hands shaking.

"What's wrong?" asked Grimm, his arms elbow deep in suds as he washed a pile of dirty dishes.

"Gabriel," said Ignatius. "There's something wrong with Gabriel. The village is crying."

"Let's go," said Grimm, not bothering to wipe his arms or remove his apron.

With gathering panic they ran from the vicarage, past the sleeping gargoyles, and into the churchyard. In horror they saw the door to the angel's cottage hanging open, and at their feet a long smear of blood ran from inside the cottage and across the grass to the nearby tree line.

"Dear God," said Ignatius. "They've taken him." He rushed inside the cottage, calling out for Gabriel, but he knew in his heart it was too late. There was a thumping of feet from outside, and Jonathan, Cay, and Elgar burst in.

"Grandfather!" Jonathan cried out.

"We saw you running," said Elgar. "What's happened?"

Ignatius could only stare helplessly at Jonathan. "I . . ." he croaked.

Jonathan launched himself up the stairs to Gabriel's workroom, trying not to look at the drying trail of crimson that marked the wooden steps. He emerged into the attic to see the scattered books, the shattered skylight, and the dusting of broken glass. Of Gabriel there was no sign.

He stood next to the workbench and gripped the edge as hard as he could to stop himself from falling. He felt faint, and the room spun around him. "This isn't fair," he said. "You take my mom and dad, and now you take my grandfather, too. I'm going to get you, Belial. I don't know how yet, but I will. You should be scared of me, just like Rook was." He wiped his eyes with the end of his sleeve as angry tears began to spill down his face. "Don't give up," he said to himself. "There's got to be something you can do to help."

And then he saw it, sitting on the bench between his hands. It had a worn leather strap and a new glass face, but it was the same watch that Gabriel had given him before. He picked it up and fastened it to his wrist. Somehow it made him feel better, as if part of his grandfather was still there with him.

"You okay, son?" rumbled Grimm, gently placing a hand on Jonathan's shoulder.

Jonathan turned to look at his friend and nodded. "We're going to get Belial, aren't we?"

"Hell, yes!" said Grimm. "We are now officially at war. Belial will rue the day he took on this village."

"But how do you fight an archdemon?" Jonathan asked.

"You've not seen what I can do with a cricket bat," said Grimm. "Now, we all need to get back to the vicarage. We need to decide what to do next."

A thought suddenly occurred to Jonathan. "The Corvidae must have been watching Gabriel. They knew what he was doing—building a key to get me into Heaven. That's why they took him, isn't it? Do you think they were waiting for him to finish it so they could take it?"

Grimm scanned the room. "I don't know, Jonathan. But if they have got the clock, then they'll also need Gabriel to show them how to use it, and that is something he's not going to do, not without a fight."

"And if they didn't find the clock?"

"Then they'll use Gabriel as a hostage to get us to hand it—and you—over to them, and that's not going to happen either."

"You won't truly hand me over to Belial, will you?"

Grimm kneeled down in front of Jonathan, still dwarfing him with his bulk. "We're a family here in

Hobbes End," he said. "We look after each other, and, by God, I'll breathe my last before I stand by and let some maniac archdemon hurt my family. I swear it, lad."

Jonathan nodded and gave Grimm a hug, his arms not even coming close to reaching round his barrel chest.

"We good?" asked Grimm.

Jonathan nodded.

"Then let's get back to the vicarage. It's time we got ready to fight, and I have Isobel ready and waiting in the garage."

"Isobel?" asked Jonathan.

"My cricket bat," said Grimm. "She's a beauty, and she's itching to kick some Corvidae butt."

Jonathan smiled in spite of himself. As long as he had Grimm and Ignatius, Cay and Elgar, Monty and Stubbs, he was not alone. He had family.

"Let's go," he said.

"Well done, Rook," said Belial. "Put him in that chair, then tie him up."

Gabriel gave a low moan.

"Ah, our guest appears to be awake," said Belial, walking over to where the angel sat slumped. He bent over and grasped Gabriel's chin, roughly raising his head.

"Now, old man," he hissed, "not only is your grandson of great interest, but Rook tells me you've built a clock that gives direct access to Heaven itself."

Gabriel glared at Belial but said nothing.

"Where have you hidden your clock? Rook mumbled something about a desert and a disappearing door."

"I built that clock to keep my grandson safe," said Gabriel. "I would die before I handed it over to you. I may have left Heaven, but I will not betray it by letting you march your armies in through a back door."

"Of course you wouldn't," said Belial. "I'm well aware that you would cease breathing before you did that. So I'm going to give you a little nudge."

"Like what?"

"You'll see." Belial grinned. "Oh, just so you know, your son wasn't very cooperative. We had to hurt him rather badly before he gave us the information we needed."

"Where is Darriel? Where is my son?" asked Gabriel, his face grim.

"Oh, we left his mangled body on the steps of Heaven as an example of what happens to those who oppose me."

"Damn you!" Gabriel spat.

"Anyhow," Belial continued, "I'm surprised you

haven't asked how my servants can enter and leave your precious village without lighting up like Roman candles."

Gabriel's eyes betrayed his curiosity. "How?" he asked.

Belial's shoulders heaved up and down as he gave a deep, rasping laugh. "Let's just say that your fall from grace had unforeseen consequences. Now, for the last time, will you be a good angel and tell me where you've hidden your clock?"

"No."

"I see," said Belial. "Well, you seem rather fond of that little girl. Cay, isn't it . . . ?"

Gabriel stared in horror.

"Yes, it's what's called an incentive to cooperate," said Belial. "Tomorrow afternoon, Rook, Raven, and Crow are going to pay Hobbes End a final visit. Once they return I think you'll feel far more obliging. You'll be begging your grandson to go fetch your clock from wherever you've hidden it and ask him to bring it to me himself."

"*No!*" screamed Gabriel, thrashing against the rope that tied him to the chair. "*You hurt Cay and you'll burn! You hear me? BURN!*"

"Oh, scary!" mocked Belial. "Will the big, bad arch-

angel manifest his wings and punish me for my impu-
dence?" He watched as Gabriel struggled in vain to free
himself. "I thought not! Take him away, Crow."

Ignoring the screaming angel as he was dragged from
the room still tied to the chair, Belial gazed out the window and into the dark.

"What do we do about those gargoyles?" asked
Raven.

"Oh, yes," said Belial mockingly. "Your little friends.
I wouldn't worry too much about them. They're just
constructs and rather rudimentary ones from the sound
of it. After that incident at the lake they'll need time to
recharge. Until then they'll be useless." Raven snorted
her contempt.

"I suggest you go get some rest," said Belial, a terrible smile crawling its way across the mottled skin of his
face. "We have a very busy day tomorrow, a very busy
day indeed."

Chapter 15
THE BATTLE OF HOBBES END

Early the following morning, Jonathan and Elgar sat in the vicarage kitchen having tea and toast. The cat could see Jonathan was desperately unhappy after Gabriel's abduction and tried to cheer him up.

"What do you call someone who's half angel, half demon?" he asked. "A dangel? An aemon?"

Jonathan smiled wearily and scratched Elgar behind the ears. "I don't know, cat," he said. "I guess we'll have to invent something."

"I quite like *dangel*," said Elgar.

Jonathan fell silent again.

"We'll find a way to rescue Gabriel and your dad. You'll see," said Elgar.

"I hope so," said Jonathan. "I really hope so."

Ignatius stuck his head round the kitchen door. He looked exhausted. "I spent all night going through the journals of my predecessors to see if I can find out how the Corvidae are getting into the village, but it's taking longer than I thought. I can't think of any way to assist Gabriel until Belial lets his demands be known, so would you come and give me a hand?"

Glad to be able to do something to help, Jonathan and Elgar followed Ignatius into his study. There were easy chairs positioned on either side of the fireplace, and between them a low table supported a chessboard on which a half-played game waited to be finished. There was a gilt-edged mirror hanging on the chimney breast, a walnut roll-top desk set against one wall, and a glass-fronted bookcase in the far corner. The bookcase was open, and a pile of leather-bound journals lay on the floor.

"How far back do they go?" asked Jonathan.

"The seventeenth century," said Ignatius. "Augustus Crumb's is the first one, although he can get a bit excitable. Then again, he was still getting used to having had an angel crash-land outside his house!"

"Any idea what we're looking for?"

Ignatius frowned. "Not really," he said. "Just anything that relates to the village defenses and how they could be breached. Right, there are just three journals left. Jonathan, would you have a look through Frederick's? He was my great-grandfather. I'll look through Sebastian's — he was my grandfather. And Elgar, you —"

"Sit here and supervise Jonathan," said the cat, waving his paws in the air. "How can I turn the pages without opposable thumbs?"

Ignatius rolled his eyes but decided it was pointless trying to argue. "Then I shall leave my father's journal till later," he sighed.

For the rest of the morning Jonathan pored over page after page of notes, diary entries, anecdotes, and strange doodles. The journals were fascinating, though, and Jonathan wished he had more time to spend getting to know this new world through these thoughts of the men who had guarded it since Gabriel fell; he promised himself that when this was all over he would do just that.

He flicked over a page near the back of Frederick's journal and with wide eyes saw a series of diagrams that looked very familiar indeed.

"Is this Monty and Stubbs?" he asked, holding the pages out for Ignatius to see.

"Oh, yes! I'm so used to them, I forgot they're a relatively recent addition. My great-grandfather was a bit of a scientist, and he loved the idea of having animated gargoyles keeping an eye on things if he wasn't around. So, after much experimentation, and with a little help from Gabriel, the boys arrived."

"And what joy they have brought to our lives." Elgar sighed.

"You're just jealous that you can't fly," said Ignatius.

"Well, yes, to be honest," said the cat.

"I bet Frederick was proud of them," said Jonathan.

"He was," said Ignatius. "So proud, he started working on something even bigger and got a bit careless. One explosion later and the east side of the vicarage, along with most of Frederick, ended up adorning the west side of the church—he had a very small coffin at his funeral. Still, in Monty and Stubbs, old Fred left us a legacy that helped save Cay, so respect is due. Unfortunately I'd forgotten how much rest the boys need after exerting themselves like that. They'll be fast asleep just when we could really use them to keep an eye out for anything in a bowler hat." He shut Frederick's journal, sighed heavily, and looked out the window. "Sometimes it's a tough job looking after this village."

"Has someone in your family always been the vicar of Hobbes End?" asked Jonathan.

Ignatius nodded. "Ever since Augustus Crumb waded into the boiling water of the village pond and dragged

Gabriel to safety. He was a brave one, Augustus. Everyone else just ran away, frightened out of their wits, but not him. He knew an angel when he saw one. There was an unforeseen bonus, though."

"What was that?"

"Well, with all that divine power flowing out of Gabriel and into the pond, Augustus absorbed some of it too. Since then, all the vicars of Hobbes End have had an affinity with the village. Just like Gabriel, we can feel when the village is happy or upset. It's not like a conversation, more like these really strong images that suddenly pop up in your head. It's how I knew that Cay was in danger at the lake, and that Gabriel had been attacked." Ignatius sighed and rubbed his eyes. "Since Augustus, both the position of vicar and the power that goes with it followed father to son, right up to the present day. It ends with me, though; I don't know who comes next."

He bowed his head, and Jonathan knew what he was referring to. "I'm sorry about what happened to your wife and son," he said softly.

Ignatius nodded and gave Jonathan a sad smile. "Thank you," he said. "And I'm so very sorry about what's happening to your family right now, Jonathan. We will find a way to defeat Belial, I promise you. Okay, let's clear these away and have a cup of tea."

As Ignatius began placing the journals back in the bookcase, Jonathan caught sight of a long mahogany box tucked away on the bottom shelf.

"What's that?" he asked.

Ignatius looked at the box and smiled. "That," he said, "is my fencing rapier. The father of an old school friend of mine is a superb weaponsmith, and he made the sword for me when I became vicar. I have an overwhelming desire to stick it into one of the Corvidae!"

"Would that hurt them? They're demons."

"They may be demons, Jonathan, but they can still bleed, and they can still die. They can't stop the village lending me the strength and speed to do what's needed. Another perk of being vicar!"

Jonathan smiled. "How about Grimm? Does he get any special powers because he was born here?"

Ignatius chuckled. "I have absolutely no idea. Then again, I'm not sure he would need any. He was born a warrior. Right. To the kitchen."

Jonathan nodded and turned to leave. As he did so, he noticed an uncharacteristic bulge behind the breast pocket of Ignatius's jacket. "What's that?" he asked.

Ignatius twitched his lapel aside to reveal an ancient leather shoulder holster. Inside it was the blue-gray steel of a pistol. "It's my grandfather Sebastian's old army revolver," he explained. "I'm not a fan of firearms myself, but right now we need all the help we can get."

"Are you a good shot?"

"Very," said Ignatius. "Although I'm better with my rapier."

Jonathan's eyes widened in surprise.

"I know," said Ignatius, almost embarrassed. "Vicars are supposed to be all bookish and dull, not run around fighting evil with a Toledo-steel rapier and a forty-five caliber Webley revolver."

Jonathan smiled. There was far more to the vicar of Hobbes End than he'd realized. "I don't think you're dull or bookish," he said. "Thank you for protecting me."

Ignatius gave Jonathan a shy grin. "It's what I do," he said.

Jonathan surprised Ignatius by stepping back into the room and hugging him, just as he had Grimm the previous day. "When this is all over, when we've found Gabriel and Mom and Dad, can I live here in the village with them?" he asked.

Ignatius paused, a lump in his throat. He looked at the small, silver-framed photograph of his wife and son that sat on a corner of his desk. "I'd like that, Jonathan," he replied. "I'd like that very much. Now, let's have a cup of tea and I'll walk you over to see Cay. I'll go through my father's journal later."

The sun hung low in the sky when the attack began. Leaving the black Rolls-Royce at the entrance to Hobbes End, Rook, Raven, and Crow marched along the forest road. They could sense the village looking for them, but they didn't care.

Rook turned to his sister. "How are the injuries to your shoulder?" he asked.

"I'll survive. I always do."

Crow grunted in admiration but said nothing; he loped alongside his siblings, his hulking frame stooped to the point that his knuckles almost touched the ground.

"That temper of yours will be your undoing, sister dear," chided Rook. "Keep yourself focused on the job at hand."

"Concentrate on your own job, brother dear," said Raven, her voice caustic. "Unless you want me to show you how it's done?"

Knowing what was at stake, Rook decided not to rise to the bait. Failure was not an option. They continued their journey in silence; in front of them lay Hobbes End, and it was completely defenseless.

Dressed in his usual shirt and suspenders, Grimm stood in the vicarage garden and took a practice swing with his cricket bat.

"I've had this since I was at school." He sighed happily. "I named it Isobel, after my first girlfriend."

"You are so odd sometimes, Grimm," said Elgar.

"I think she needs more linseed oil, though. The wood's starting to dry out." He took another swing, unaware that Rook was standing atop the garden wall. The demon was just a silhouette against the sun, all bowler hat and razor-sharp talons.

"Hello, cat," hissed Rook, his empty face staring at Elgar.

"Ahh! Grimm!" shouted Elgar, diving into the shrubbery.

Unfazed by the sudden appearance of the demon, Grimm turned to face him. "Nice hat!" he said calmly. "Mind if I add it to my collection?"

"You can try," said Rook, jumping from the wall. "But you'll probably end up dead. Everybody else has!"

"Well, aren't you the big man?" said Grimm, letting Isobel drop to the grass. "Take your best shot."

Rook snorted, then with incredible speed leaped at Grimm. Elgar put his paws over his eyes, sure that his friend was going to be torn to pieces, but Grimm stayed motionless, stoically ignoring Rook and his threats. There was retribution to be handed out, and he was just the man to do it. The second before Rook's talons touched his shirt, Grimm braced himself on his back foot and delivered a punch to the demon's face that would have floored an elephant.

"That's for Jonathan!" shouted Grimm, before delivering another punch, an uppercut that lifted Rook completely off his feet and sent him reeling across the lawn. "And that's for Cay!"

The demon's bowler hat flew off as he landed in a surprised heap near the shrubbery.

"You dare!" shrieked Rook, struggling to his feet.

"Oh, I dare all right," said Grimm, picking up the fallen hat and placing it on his head. "I've been wanting a private chat with you." Retrieving Isobel, he took another practice swing. "Excellent balance," he said. "You'll do nicely, my lovely." He turned back to the dazed Rook and smiled. "Right, then. Where were we?"

Isobel at the ready, he launched himself at the demon . . .

Ignatius sat at his writing desk studying his father's journal. He'd barely begun reading when a prickling at the back of his neck signaled that something was wrong. Jumping to his feet, he looked over his shoulder just as the study window erupted in a shower of wood and glass. Crouched on the ruined sill was Raven, her long black hair streaming out from beneath her bowler hat.

"Reverend Crumb, I presume?" she hissed.

"Unfortunately for you, yes," replied Ignatius. His movements a blur, he drew, aimed, and fired his grandfather's old army revolver.

The bullet struck Raven in her left shoulder and tore through the wound already inflicted by Cay's father — the impact knocking her out the window and onto the front lawn. Incredibly, her hat stayed on.

Ignatius sighed and looked at the pistol in his hand, a thin curl of smoke trickling from the end of the barrel. "I'll finish this the gentleman's way, I think," he said, tucking the revolver back into the shoulder holster under his jacket. Squatting in front of his bookcase, he slid out the long mahogany box, flipped the catches at each end, and opened the lid to reveal a rapier forged from the finest Toledo steel and wrapped in red velvet.

Wrenching open the front door of the vicarage, Ignatius strode out to meet Raven, sword in hand . . .

Jonathan sat on the windowsill in Cay's bedroom, deep in thought and nursing a mug of tea. Cay was lying on her bed, her nose deep in a book. Try as he might, Jonathan just couldn't understand how the Corvidae could get into Hobbes End when the village should be able to detect and incinerate them.

He was missing something obvious, he knew, but exactly *what* kept eluding him. It was then that he remembered the article in the *Times* from three days before — the piece about the theft of the meteorite. Snippets of information poured together, blended, arranged themselves into the correct order, and Jonathan realized he might have the answer. He remembered his grandfather's words at dinner when he had spoken about his fall: *I threw myself from the gates of Heaven and let my wings burn as I fell. I no longer wanted to be an angel; I just wanted to be Gabriel and to be left alone. So on the second of September 1666 I crash-landed here, in a little hamlet in the middle of a forest.*

"The second of September 1666," Jonathan said under his breath, remembering sitting at the kitchen table with his mother and the history books he'd loved reading. "Gabriel arrived the same night the Great Fire of London started. His wings burned as he fell. What if it wasn't a meteorite that started the fire? What if it was a burning piece of his wings? If Belial and the Corvidae knew what the meteorite actually was and stole it from the British Museum, maybe they're using it to hide themselves from Hobbes End."

He hopped off the windowsill and walked to the bedroom door. "I'll be back in a minute," he called over his shoulder to Cay.

"Hmm?" she mumbled.

"I've got to see Ignatius, I've just thought of something. I'll tell you when I get back if it's not just a daft idea."

She nodded and carried on reading her book while Jonathan shut the bedroom door behind him and ran downstairs into the shop. He froze at the sight of Kenneth Forrester sprawled unconscious on the floor. Next to him stood a grotesque, simian figure in a pinstriped suit and bowler hat, a bloodied rolling pin clutched in one hand.

"Afternoon," snarled Crow.

Jonathan turned and sprinted down the hallway to the kitchen. He barely had time to see the prone figure of Mrs. Forrester before tripping over her outstretched legs and falling headlong. Scrambling to his feet, he saw Crow's bulk moving purposefully toward him, and he thought about Cay, unaware and defenseless upstairs — he didn't want to lead the demon to her.

If he's after me, thought Jonathan, *then he'll have to catch me first!* Without hesitation, he bolted for the back door . . .

Rook and Grimm stood toe to toe, beating the hell out of each other. Elgar watched open-mouthed as the powerhouse that was Halcyon Nathaniel Oberon Grimm ducked and whirled like a dancer, using Isobel to give Rook an absolute thrashing. The demon's suit was in tatters, and the skin that covered his body was torn and rent. Black ichor dripped from the wounds, and where it fell the grass rapidly turned brown.

Grimm didn't remain unscathed, however. Time and again Rook's razor-sharp talons struck home, shredding his shirt and leaving deep cuts across his chest that bled profusely. Elgar desperately wanted to help Grimm but couldn't see an opportunity to grab hold of Rook's leg without being battered to a pulp.

A pistol shot rang out from inside the vicarage, and Grimm felt a moment of panic. *The other Corvidae are here as well,* he thought to himself. *I've got to finish this quickly.* Standing up straight, he placed Isobel over one meaty shoulder and pulled a handkerchief from his trouser pocket. Mopping blood and sweat from his face, he grinned widely at Rook. "Are we having fun yet?" he asked.

"Are you insane, human?" asked Rook. "I'm the leader of the Corvidae, I'm a nightmare made flesh, I—"

"Oh, stop banging on and answer the damn question!" barked Grimm. "Are we having fun yet?"

Rook's temper finally snapped. With unnatural speed and ferocity he lashed out at Grimm's throat. Grimm saw the blow coming and sidestepped to his right, grunting in pain as Rook's talons gouged furrows across his shoulder. But with Rook now off balance, Grimm used all his strength to swing Isobel in a wide arc, striking the back of the demon's neck with bone-crushing force. The blow spun Rook round like a top, tearing from around his neck a small glass vial on a metal chain. Elgar watched as the vial sailed through the air and connected solidly with the wall of the vicarage. It shattered.

Isobel, unused to being swung so violently, snapped clean in two, leaving just the handle in Grimm's hands. The body of the bat went flying into a mulberry bush, narrowly missing Elgar.

Grimm looked stunned. *"Isobel!"* he cried.

"Forget about the bat, you lump!" Elgar shouted. "What's happening to Rook?"

Grimm stared in amazement as the demon's body began to shake and convulse, smoke pouring from beneath the ruined suit. With a terrible shriek, Rook stumbled toward the open gate in the garden wall . . .

Raven got to her feet just in time to receive the keen edge of a rapier across her cheek. Hissing with rage, she jabbed a clawed hand straight at Ignatius's eyes. With the innate grace and balance of a trained swordsman, he leaned back just far enough to avoid her talons while aiming another blow at her head. This time he succeeded in slicing off her left ear.

Howling with pain, Raven clapped a hand to the injury and dived away from Ignatius. He followed her across the grass, sword at the ready. The vicar of Hobbes End could feel the village supporting him, cheering him on, filling him with the strength he needed.

"How dare you attack my village!" he screamed at the demon. *"How dare you hurt a child!"*

He lowered the tip of his rapier, desperate to regain control of his emotions. Raven snarled and lashed out with her foot, knocking Ignatius off balance. Before he could retaliate, she raked her talons across his shin and dashed away toward the open gates.

Gritting his teeth against the pain, Ignatius ignored the warm, wet feeling building up in his shoe and sped after her. He reached the vicarage gates and hammered on the nearest post to try to wake Stubbs, but the gargoyle was dead to the world.

"Damn it!" he cursed, limping after Raven. "Looks like it's just you and me . . ."

Jonathan felt a clawed hand dig into his shoulder as Crow wrenched him away from the door.

"No point running," said Crow, throwing Jonathan across the kitchen table. "Not from me."

"You animal!" spat Jonathan, struggling to his feet beside the stunned body of Mrs. Forrester. A livid bruise on her temple showed where Crow had struck her.

"Not animal, just monster!" gurgled Crow happily. "Now sit still while I hit you. Then I can go get the girl."

Jonathan's eyes widened as he fully understood that Crow didn't want him. He was after Cay! But he was no longer the powerless boy he had been. In his anger he ignored Gabriel's warning and reached for what lay inside him. Crouching at the back of his mind and eager to be free, a tidal wave of power rushed to answer Jonathan's summons.

Absolute agony tore through his body as a mass of purple light erupted from his back, then split into hundreds of ribbons, their edges serrated like steak knives. They moved independently of each other as if alive; inside them flowed a never-ending stream of mathematical symbols, quantum equations so complex, they were beyond comprehension.

He sank shaking to his knees as the voice screamed

inside him, just like it had when he'd faced Rook. "This abomination is not your equal! Rend it! Tear it! Burn it!" With mounting horror, Jonathan found he had absolutely no control over what he had unleashed.

Undeterred by Jonathan's wings, Crow reached for him with arms the size of a gorilla's. It was a mistake he'd live to regret, for like a nest of cobras, Jonathan's wing ribbons launched themselves at Crow. Half of them wrapped themselves round the demon's massive body; the others wrapped themselves round Crow's right wrist. Then they pulled themselves in opposite directions.

"Oh God, no!" cried Jonathan as he saw what he — his wings — was doing. "Stop it!"

Crow was lifted clean off his feet and slammed into the ceiling. As plaster and wood rained down all Jonathan could think of was his father's sacrifice, how he'd dropped an entire cottage on himself to save his wife and son. Fury suddenly raged through him as every frustrated, powerless minute of the last few weeks flashed through his mind. These things had taken everything from him — his parents, his home, his grandfather, his whole damn life. The power inside him knew it; it responded to his anger, and it wanted its pound of flesh. Now he could only watch dumbly as his wings pulled even harder.

Crow opened his awful mouth and let out a scream that sounded like a wounded animal. The voice inside Jonathan exulted in such exquisite vengeance, then tore Crow's right arm clean off at the shoulder.

"*No!*" cried Jonathan. "Grandfather, help me!" But deep down he knew he was on his own. The genie was out of the bottle, and it could kill him even as it tried to save him.

Black blood poured from the wounded Crow as he thrashed in the grip of Jonathan's wings. Finished with the demon's arm, the ribbons made to wrap themselves round Crow's throat. All Jonathan could feel was pain and anger — he wished desperately for all this to stop, but his wings wouldn't listen . . .

"Jonathan!" screamed Cay as she appeared in the kitchen door.

He looked at her and saw absolute horror in her face. It wasn't Crow she was looking at; it was him — at what he had become.

I'm a monster, he thought, and with this realization his wings simply winked out of existence like a snuffed candle.

The wounded Crow dropped to the floor and swung round to grab Cay with his remaining arm. She shrieked and pounded at the demon with all her strength, but Crow seemed oblivious. Leaving the dazed Jonathan kneeling and retching on the kitchen floor, the Corvidae smashed through the back door, dragging the terrified Cay with him . . .

Ignatius watched as Raven stumbled onto the narrow earthen bank that dammed one side of the village pond. He knew she couldn't outrun him—the pain and blood loss from her injuries must have weakened her. Glancing at the cottages that bordered the green, Ignatius could see faces at windows, doors opening.

"*Stay inside!*" he bellowed as Angus McFadden started to leave his cottage, a poker in his hand. Ignatius knew that if he didn't stop them, every inhabitant of Hobbes End would try to come to his aid and probably get themselves torn to pieces doing it. Around the corner by the church rushed Professor Morgenstern, clutching a box of what may well have been his homemade hand grenades.

"*No!*" Ignatius shouted as he ran. "*This is my fight!*"

The villagers looked on in horrified indecision as Ignatius plowed onward toward Raven.

The demon reached the middle of the dam and stopped, steadying herself on the wheel that worked the sluice gate. With obvious effort she forced herself upright, adjusting her bowler hat as she turned to face her pursuer.

With careful steps Ignatius followed Raven onto the dam, stopping just outside her reach. He raised his sword to his forehead in a grim salute.

"It looks like we have an audience," hissed Raven, nodding at the villagers as they hesitantly stood at the far edge of the green, wanting to do something but unsure how to help.

"It's their home you've invaded," snarled Ignatius. "They get to see your punishment." With blinding speed he thrust at Raven's shoulder, aiming for where he'd shot her. She screamed in agony as the rapier hit home, piercing deeply into her flesh. Enraged, the demon swung wildly at Ignatius, one of her talons opening a gash across his forehead.

"*Damn!*" he shouted, trying to stop blood flowing into his eyes. Raven gave a gurgling, inhuman chuckle, then taunted Ignatius by licking his blood from her hand.

A scream erupted from behind the village shop. It sounded like a young girl.

"*Cay!*" said Ignatius, and he instinctively turned to look. It was all the opening that Raven needed. With a hiss, she swung her fist and caught him a terrible blow to the side of the head.

The world spun, and Ignatius dropped to the ground as if poleaxed. His rapier slipped from his fingers, and he watched in despair as it rolled off the dam and into the dark water of the pond. With a splash, the sword was gone.

Raven pushed the dazed Ignatius onto his back, crouching astride him and pinning his arms with her knees. He fought for breath and tried with all his fading might to tear himself from Raven's grasp, and he could feel the village doing all it could to help him, but she was too strong.

"Now, little man," hissed Raven, "let me show you what I dare to do!" With deliberate, almost theatrical slowness, she raised her hand in order to strike him dead . . .

Elgar shot from his hiding place and struck the garden gate head on, slamming it shut in front of Rook.

The demon smashed into the now-closed gate, almost tearing it from its hinges. Unfortunately for Rook they held, and he glared at Elgar through a cloud of smoke.

"Traitor," he hissed.

"Yep," said Elgar. "Looks that way, doesn't it?"

Still clutching Isobel's handle, Grimm watched aghast as Rook began hammering at the gate, only to stop and give vent to one final, terrible howl. Then he burst into flames.

The tattered suit went first. Then his skin peeled away to reveal the scaly humanoid form of the demon beneath. It was absolutely horrible. Within seconds Rook was reduced to nothing more than a pile of ash, staining the lawn a diseased black.

Grimm and Elgar stood open-mouthed until the sound of people shouting snapped them back to reality.

"Oh, hell!" shouted Grimm. "Come on, cat, we're not finished yet!"

They ran as fast as they could from the garden, vaulting over Rook's remains and thundering down the drive. Clearing the main gates, they could see Ignatius pinned to the ground by Raven, her hand raised to strike.

From the other side of the green the villagers, led by Angus McFadden, were charging round toward the dam. Fast as he was, Grimm knew that neither he nor Angus would get to Ignatius in time.

"*Run, cat!*" he shouted.

Not needing further encouragement, Elgar dropped his head low and streaked across the green like a furry black missile. Without breaking stride, Grimm voiced a quick and silent prayer, then threw Isobel's handle with all his might.

Just as Raven's taloned hand began its descent, Isobel's remains struck her square on the back of the head, knocking her bowler hat off and into the pond. With a roar she swung herself around, only to hear the shout of *"Incoming!"* for the second time that week.

A ball of fury hit her full in the face and began biting and scratching for all he was worth. Screeching in pain, Raven had to use both hands to get hold of Elgar and fling him away. She turned back to Ignatius. It was then she saw that while she struggled with Elgar, the vicar had managed to free his right hand from beneath her knee. Pressed against her chest, right next to her rotten heart, was the hard steel muzzle of an old Webley revolver.

Demon and cleric stared impassively at each other. Then Ignatius pulled the trigger.

There was a muffled report, and Raven's body jerked backward. Her hands dropped to her sides, and she stared in disbelief at the smoking hole in her breast pocket. Black blood trickled from the corner of her mouth, and with an almost human sigh she toppled from the dam to land with a splash in the pond.

Ignatius lay back on the damp earth, blood in his eyes and Sebastian's old revolver still clutched in his hand. He wasn't sure whether to laugh or cry. A moment later he felt a weight on his chest and a cold wet nose pressed up against his. There was a faint aroma of kippers.

"You all right?" asked Elgar.

"Yes, cat," said Ignatius, a lump in his throat as he gently stroked the fur on Elgar's back. "I'm all right."

A shaking of the earth signaled Grimm's approach, closely followed by that of Angus and the rest of the villagers.

"You still alive in there?" boomed Grimm, a daft grin plastered across his face.

"Aye, are ye hurt?" asked Angus.

Too overcome to speak, Ignatius let Grimm help him to his feet.

"Elgar and I got jumped by Rook," said Grimm. "But he's been reduced to a stain on the back lawn. And as for Raven . . ."

They looked at the demon's body as it floated facedown in the pond below, bowler hat bobbing next to her in the water.

"Um . . ." said Elgar.

"What's wrong?" asked Ignatius.

"Well, not wanting to pee on your chips, Zorro," said Elgar, "but aren't there three of these things?"

Before anyone could respond, they heard a cry from the direction of the village shop. Turning to look, they saw Mr. and Mrs. Flynn half dragging Jonathan toward them. His clothing was torn, and he had blood on his face.

"They've got Cay," he cried out. "They've got Cay!"

Chapter 16

WAR WOUNDS

It was almost midnight, and the vicarage bore a startling resemblance to a military field hospital. Upstairs, Kenneth and Joanne Forrester were staying in Ignatius's room. Kenneth had been knocked unconscious, but apart from a large lump on his forehead his lupine constitution ensured his quick recovery. Joanne was a different matter entirely, and it wasn't until she opened her eyes that Grimm decided not to take her to the local hospital. Joanne's silent distress over Cay's abduction was painfully obvious however, and the pleading on her face as she held Kenneth's hand came close to breaking Grimm's heart.

"Let's have a look at that shoulder, old boy," said Ignatius, forcing Grimm to take a seat in the kitchen.

Grimm grumbled but let his friend apply badly needed antiseptic and bandages to his chest and shoulder.

"Did you manage to open the sluice gate?" asked Ignatius.

"Yep," said Grimm. "The pond should be empty by morning."

"Excellent. And did you retrieve Raven's corpse?"

"Well, sort of. I was checking the body when I found something on a chain round her neck. No sooner had I unfastened it than her body burst into flames. It looks like the one Rook was wearing before I knocked it off him. Come to think of it, he caught fire shortly afterward too. I think it confirms Jonathan's theory."

"What does?" asked Jonathan, walking into the kitchen and slumping wearily into a chair.

"This vial," said Ignatius, holding it up to the light and peering at the tiny black shard inside. "You figured it out, my boy. You figured out how the Corvidae could get in. Very well done."

"So they were using pieces of Gabriel's wings to shield themselves?" asked Jonathan.

Ignatius nodded. "Belial could never enter Hobbes End himself—there's no hiding the power of an archdemon—but the Corvidae are a different matter. Belial must have known what the meteorite really was, so he stole it and used it to hide what he was up to."

Grimm frowned. "But how did a bit of Gabriel's wings hide the Corvidae from the village?"

"It's deceptively simple," said Ignatius. "The wing is the angel, the angel is the wing. There is no difference. Hobbes End is sentient because so much of Gabriel's power is here, burned into the earth beneath the pond. Just like his wings, Hobbes End is part of him. When the Corvidae wore these vials containing fragments of his wings, they were hidden beneath a cloak of grace. No wonder the village was so uneasy; it could sense the Corvidae but it just couldn't see them!" He opened the vial and tipped the contents into his hand. They all peered at what looked like a small sliver of charcoal, then gasped as it crumbled to dust in front of their eyes.

"What just happened?" asked Jonathan.

"Hobbes End has taken Gabriel's power back," said Ignatius. "It couldn't see the demons while they had possession of these fragments, but it gradually sucked the power from them. The Corvidae would have had to replace them each time they came back here."

"Do you think they've run out of meteorite?" asked Grimm.

"I don't think it matters now," said Ignatius. "Two of the Corvidae are dead, and Crow isn't going to come back in a hurry, nor does he need to. Belial has the leverage he requires."

Jonathan went pale at the thought of Cay being used as a hostage, as a bargaining chip.

"Are you all right?" asked Grimm.

"No," said Jonathan. "I lost control yesterday and it almost killed me." He bit his lip. "And I just keep seeing Cay's face when she saw what I'd done to Crow. So Belial's taken my entire family, and now he's taken my friend too. I just don't know what to do. I want to help, but I daren't use my wings again—it's too dangerous. The thought of Cay being hurt and alone, though, makes me feel sick."

"We know, Jonathan," Ignatius reassured him. "But there's nothing we can do now apart from get patched up and wait. Belial wants something, and I bet we find out what it is very soon."

"Why didn't Crow take me, too?" asked Jonathan. "I was in so much pain, I couldn't fight back. I thought Belial wanted me."

Ignatius paused in his bandaging of Grimm's shoulder and stared at Jonathan. "You're right," he said. "That is strange. Why would he take Cay when he could easily have taken you? Belial won't have given up on his plans, so why leave you behind, unless . . . ?"

"Unless what?" said Jonathan.

"Unless Belial needs you here," said Ignatius, his brow furrowed in thought.

"There's only one thing it could be," said Jonathan. "He knows about my grandfather's clock—the key he was building to let me into Heaven. Belial doesn't just want me, he wants a way into Heaven too! The Corvidae have been lurking about, listening and watching, so they found out what Gabriel was building and waited for him to finish it before they took him."

"But they didn't manage to get hold of it?" said Ignatius. "Perhaps Gabriel managed to hide it from them somehow. Hide it somewhere that they can't go."

"Like somewhere that only an angel can get to," said Elgar, vigorously cleaning Rook's dusty remains from his ears with a cotton bud.

"Or someone with angelic blood, maybe?" said Ignatius.

Jonathan put his head in his hands as everything fell into place. "That's why they took Cay, isn't it? She's a hostage. With Belial holding my dad, and Gabriel and Cay prisoner, he knows that I'll do whatever he wants. I don't have a choice."

Ignatius put a reassuring hand on Jonathan's shoulder. "I think that's the likely explanation, but we have to wait. The fact that Belial may want something from you gives us time to figure out how to beat him."

Jonathan nodded, but he was at a loss as to how they

would save Cay, Gabriel, and his father. Belial seemed to be ahead of them every step of the way.

"I hope my mom's managed to get to Lucifer," he said. "At least she'll be safe."

"We can but hope, Jonathan," said Ignatius. "We can but hope."

Jonathan nodded, but he felt more empty than he'd thought possible.

"Right, then," said Ignatius. "Grimm, would you please attend to my leg before I pass out from loss of blood?" Swapping seats, he gingerly placed his foot on a spare chair while, with the aid of adhesive stitches and a lot of gauze, Grimm began fixing the mess Raven had made of Ignatius's leg.

"Oh, that reminds me," Grimm said, turning to look at the cat. "Rook recognized you before he exploded. Called you a traitor. What was all that about?"

"Well, it's like this," said Elgar, raising a paw for emphasis. "I'm not—"

"Not really a cat," said Ignatius. "Haven't either of you figured that out yet?"

An astonished silence was his response.

"I guess that means no. Come here, Elgar." Ignatius pointed to his outstretched legs. "Just mind my war wounds, if you please."

"Here we go!" said Elgar. With great reluctance he clambered out of the sink and walked over to sit on Ignatius's lap. "I'll get my things," he offered. "I haven't got much. Just an old chew toy and a packet of kippers in the fridge."

"Oh, stop it!" said Ignatius, tapping Elgar gently on the nose. "You know very well that I wouldn't send you away, little demon. You're like family after all this time."

Gasps erupted from Jonathan and Grimm.

"Oh, great! Now everyone knows my big secret. I may be a bit morally flexible, but I'm not evil."

"I know you're not," said Ignatius.

"Phew!" said Elgar. He paused to glare at Grimm. "What are you smiling at? I may be a demon, but I'm not like Rook. Not all demons are bad, you know. And not all angels are good. Lucifer, anyone?"

Grimm lifted both hands in a gesture of surrender. "Okay, okay, point taken. You don't have to prove yourself to me, cat. You did a cracking job today."

"Why, thank you," said Elgar, gesturing regally. "You may feed me now."

"Don't push it!" growled Grimm.

"Well, I know your story's a fascinating one, Elgar," said Ignatius, lifting the cat from his lap. "And I'm sure everyone would like to hear it. But since Grimm's finished patching me up, I'm going to get some rest. It's been a long day, and I have a feeling that tomorrow will require a clear head." He limped out of the kitchen, chuckling to himself as he went. "Whoever heard of a talking cat? Honestly!"

"Now I've heard everything," said Grimm. "More tea, anyone?"

Cay felt disoriented and sick. She'd been bound, gagged, blindfolded, and tossed over Crow's shoulder. She then suffered a long and uncomfortable trip through the forest while dangling upside down.

Her head was awhirl. What about Mom and Dad, Jonathan, and everyone else? What was going on? She tried to struggle, but the demon's one remaining arm clamped her so tightly, she began to have trouble breathing. Deciding that nothing could be gained from panic, she stopped resisting and waited to see what happened.

Eventually the demon came to a halt, and Cay felt herself lowered onto a blanket. Her hands were untied, and she heard a metallic clunk as a lid was closed above her. Ripping off her blindfold and gag, she realized that she was in a car trunk.

Shouting to be let out, she hammered on the inside of the trunk and kicked the back of the seats, but there was no response. The car pulled away, and she braced her feet against the bulkhead to stop herself from being thrown about.

The journey was interminable. Hot, half suffocated, and with painfully cramped muscles, Cay was too tired to feel anything but relief when the car finally came to a halt. She heard the sound of doors being opened and closed, then the crunch of footsteps on gravel. The trunk opened, and bright light flooded in.

With even less ceremony than before, Crow grabbed her, threw her back over his shoulder, and marched off. She hung upside down, unable to resist, as she was carried through a doorway, up a large staircase, through another door, and into what looked like a study.

Crow lifted Cay from his shoulder and stood her on her feet, but she sank to her knees, too tired to stay upright. The floor was covered with deep pile carpet, and she immediately just wanted to curl up on it and go to sleep, but all thoughts of sleeping were rudely shoved aside when the swivel chair behind the desk in front of her spun round. In it sat a tall man with the coldest eyes she'd ever seen.

"Ah, Miss Forrester, I presume?" He stepped out from behind his desk and walked up to Cay, and she felt herself trembling as a nameless fear washed through her. His face was little more than diseased tissue paper stretched tight over his skull, and here and there the skin would pulse and ripple, like cockroaches under thinly sliced ham.

Taking Cay's chin gently in his hand, the man leaned in close and looked her straight in the eyes. "I'm Belial," he said. "And you, my dear, are going to help me acquire both Jonathan and Gabriel's clock, whether you want to or not."

Cay returned Belial's stare until the stench of decay leeching from him began to choke her — it was like rotten meat being cooked on a barbecue. She knew Belial was supposed to be an archdemon, but she hadn't really given much thought to what an archdemon actually looked like. This decomposing corpse in a suit was not, however, what she'd expected.

"Where's Gabriel?" she demanded, struggling to quell the fear that filled her. "Where's Jonathan's dad? If you've hurt either of them, Jonathan's going to take you apart!"

"Well, he certainly seems to have disarmed Crow." Belial chuckled. "The boy is shaping up nicely. With him under my control there's nothing that can stand in my way, not even Lucifer. And as for my collection of angels, you'll find out about them in due course." Leaving Cay shaking with nausea and dread, he turned his attention to Crow. "I take it the absence of Rook and Raven means they underestimated the Reverend Crumb and his friends yet again?"

Crow nodded, clutching at the awful wound on his shoulder.

Belial gave a derisive snort. "Go and get patched up," he ordered. "You're dripping on the carpet."

The demon shuffled from the room, leaving the terrified Cay alone with her captor.

"Right," he said. "Follow me, Miss Forrester."

Too scared to disobey, Cay followed Belial out of his office, along a hallway, and into a well-appointed suite of rooms. Tied to a chair in front of the window was Gabriel. His body sagged in its restraints, and his long, unbound hair fell forward, hiding his face.

"I'll be back," said Belial, leaving the room and locking the door behind him.

Cay ran over to the old angel and untied the ropes that bound him. "Gabriel?" she cried, shaking his shoulder. "Gabriel, can you hear me?"

The angel slowly raised his head, as if the effort of doing so was more than he could bear, and his hair fell back to reveal a crude bandage covering the upper part of his face. The bottom of the bandage was crusted with dried blood.

"Oh God!" gasped Cay. "What has he done to you?"

Gabriel squeezed her hand and moaned. "He took

my eyes, child. He took my son, and then . . . then he took my eyes."

Squeezing his hand in return, Cay did the only thing she could for Gabriel. She wept for him.

Dawn broke over Hobbes End. On the patio, a bleary-eyed Grimm sat on an old deck chair and nursed yet another mug of hot tea. His injuries ached too much to allow him to nod off for long, so he'd decided to sit and watch the sunrise instead. Beside him, curled up on a cushion, was Elgar.

Upstairs in his room, Jonathan tossed and turned as he dreamed of Cay. She was flying her kite and kept being pulled farther and farther away from him. He tried to run after her, but his feet wouldn't move.

"Cay! Wait!" he shouted, but she was gone, leaving him alone in the dark.

Bolting upright, his chest heaving with phantom exertion, Jonathan realized that he wasn't going to be able to sleep any more. He swung his legs out of bed, wrapped himself in a blanket, and went downstairs to make himself some hot chocolate. Hearing voices outside, he peered through the window and saw Grimm and Elgar sitting on the patio. Desperately needing company, Jonathan went outside to join them.

"'Ello, 'ello," said Grimm. "Can't sleep either, eh?"

"No," said Jonathan. "I keep dreaming about Cay."

"Well, come and join us. Elgar was about to tell me how he ended up as a cat!"

Grabbing a chair from the kitchen, Jonathan perched himself next to Elgar. Cocooned in his blanket, he listened to his friends talk, relieved to have something to take his mind off Cay.

"I was just asking Elgar why he didn't tell me he was a demon when he first arrived," Grimm said.

"Because everyone thinks all demons are evil," Elgar replied sleepily. "Which is, of course, bilge. Take Jonathan's mom, for example."

"She may be a demon," said Jonathan, "but I do know she definitely isn't evil."

"Well said, lad," nodded Grimm, flexing his injured shoulder and wincing as pain shot up his arm. "But, Elgar, if the village let you in without burning you to a crisp, then why would I turn you away?"

"Oh, I don't know." The cat sighed. "After everything I'd been through I didn't want to have to keep on running."

"What were you running from?" asked Jonathan.

"I'm getting to that," said Elgar. "Look, Hell's a big place. There are umpteen different tribes covering an area that makes Heaven look like a postage stamp. Sure, you get your hordes of darkness following the archdemons around, but Hell's changing. More and more tribes are getting fed up with the constant backstabbing, fighting, and drunken dinner parties, so they're looking for an alternative."

"Such as?" asked Grimm.

"Such as the area Lucifer controls," replied Elgar. "He's not like the three archdemons; in fact, trying to figure out what's going on in his head is pointless. Lucifer's not good or evil; he's just very, very scary. Scary enough for the archdemons to leave him alone, even when they'd like nothing more than to duff him up."

"So where do you fit in?" asked Jonathan.

"Well, my parents live in the part of Hell controlled by Belial, but they wanted to leave and go to the bit controlled by Lucifer. Belial found out about this and decided to pay my family a visit, *persuade* them to stay, if you get my drift."

"That doesn't sound good," said Jonathan. "What does an archdemon like Belial look like, anyway?"

"Not the way you'd expect," said Elgar. "Demons come in all shapes and sizes. Rubbery puddles with tentacles, giant insects, funny-looking things with animal heads, and humanoid ones like my family and your mom. Belial chooses to appear human, but like he's been dead for a couple of weeks."

Jonathan swallowed hard. "What did he do to your family?" he asked.

"He sent in the Corvidae to beat my parents and big brother to a pulp for daring to challenge his authority."

"I'm so sorry, cat," said Grimm. "If I'd been there, I'd have given them what for!"

"Yeah, I know you would. Mom and Dad wanted to accept their punishment so nobody else would get hurt, but I had other ideas. I waded into the Corvidae as best I could and gave my brother time to get away. I got the stuffing beaten out of me, of course, but it was worth it. Belial was furious. He said that since I was so badly housetrained, maybe I'd enjoy life more as a pet. He turned me into a cat, which, I might add, is a very painful experience. Then he threw me out of Hell and told me that if I ever set foot inside it again, I'd be killed on sight."

"But that's awful," said Jonathan. "Do you know what happened to your family?"

"No, I don't. If my brother managed to escape, then hopefully he'll have been able to get an audience with Lucifer. There's always an outside chance that he might help. But you never know with him; fallen angels can be so testy. I thought about trying to see him myself, but I was too scared that Belial would catch me."

Jonathan and Grimm just nodded, not knowing what to say.

"So I had no option but to run, and after wandering around for a bit I found myself here. Now it seems that Belial and the Corvidae have managed to catch up with me anyway. Why does the universe insist on farting in my face every chance it gets? Anyway, thanks for killing Rook, Grimm. It gave me a real sense of . . . umm . . . what's that German word that means shameful joy?"

"*Schadenfreude?*"

"That's the one!"

Feeling sad for his friend, Jonathan scratched Elgar gently behind the ears while Grimm placed his mug of tea on the patio for the cat to have a drink.

"Do you know which part of Hell my mother comes from?" asked Jonathan.

"Nope," said Elgar. "But Hell's a very big place. My guess is that your mom's side of the family also lives in the bit controlled by Belial — it's probably how he found out about you in the first place. When this current unpleasantness is over I'll take you there, if you like. We can have a joint expedition to find our respective families. Your mom might have gotten to Lucifer's tower by now. She could have met my brother and not even know it!"

Elgar grinned impishly at Jonathan, who couldn't help but smile back.

"Blimey," said Grimm. "You couldn't make it up, could you?"

"No, not really," said Elgar. "Now please let me get some shuteye, will you? I'm pooped."

"Okay, then, cat, we'll watch over you while you sleep," said Grimm.

Elgar closed his yellow eyes and didn't let Grimm see that he was smiling.

Listening to Elgar, Jonathan realized something. Behind all his bluster the cat had a lot in common with him: he wasn't what he appeared to be, and he didn't know where his parents were either.

Chapter 17
THE WINDOWS OF MY WINGS

At nine o'clock that morning the inhabitants of the vicarage began to stir. Kenneth Forrester came downstairs, gratefully accepting morning tea and toast along with everyone else.

"I'm so worried about Cay," he said. "Joanne's frantic, and I don't know what to do."

"I'm positive they're not going to hurt her, Ken," said Ignatius. "Belial wants something, and he's going to use her as leverage to get it. Believe me, we are far from beaten yet!"

Kenneth nodded wearily. "Thank you."

"I know your cottage got damaged, so you're welcome to stay here as long as you like," said Ignatius. "Please try not to worry about Cay."

"If Belial hurts my daughter," growled Kenneth, "I'll hunt him down and gut him while he's still breathing. I'm just going to take some breakfast up to Joanne; I'll speak to you later." Placing a mug of tea and a plate of toast on a tray, he disappeared back upstairs.

"What do we do now?" Jonathan asked Ignatius.

"I know it's difficult, but we wait just a little bit longer. There's bound to be some kind of ultimatum, and then we can decide what to do. Anyway, right now I need to retrieve my rapier from the bottom of the pond."

Jonathan, Elgar, Ignatius, and Grimm stood by the vicarage gates. After repeatedly banging his fist on each gatepost, Ignatius eventually got Montgomery and Stubbs to wake up.

"Oh, we needed that sleep, didn't we, Mr. Stubbs?" said a groggy Montgomery, yawning widely.

"Indeed we did, Mr. Montgomery, indeed we did," said Stubbs, yawning even wider in response.

"I need you two to be on guard," said Ignatius. "The village was attacked yesterday while you were asleep. Miss Forrester has been kidnapped."

"Oh no!" cried Montgomery.

"I hate being a stupid sleepy gargoyle!" growled

Stubbs, his face twisted into an expression of complete anguish.

"You're not stupid, Stubbsey," said Jonathan. "Or you, Monty. You already saved Cay and her dad. Don't forget that."

"Jonathan's right, boys," said Ignatius. "This is not your fault. You can only do so much, and as far as everyone in the village is concerned you're heroes, both of you. Now, I want you to get as much rest as you can, but keep an eye out, just in case. Okay?"

The gargoyles stood to attention and saluted.

"Righto, chief," said Montgomery.

"Leave it to us," Stubbs concurred.

"Good, but no flying unless absolutely necessary, okay? You'll be sleeping for weeks at this rate."

The gargoyles nodded.

Happy that Montgomery and Stubbs would keep an eye on things, Ignatius led the way across the village green, his unlit pipe tucked into the corner of his mouth as usual.

They reached the pond that Grimm had drained the night before, and Jonathan stared in awe at what usually lay hidden beneath the dark water. While Ignatius, Grimm, and Elgar looked on in quiet respect, he stood rooted to the spot, unable to speak. The pond basin wasn't what he'd expected. Rather than a layer of mud, old bicycle wheels, and indignant frogs, he saw a wide expanse of black glass, shimmering in a flow of clear water from an underground spring. The glass was cracked and pitted in a million places, and in the center was something extraordinary—a crater with an unmistakably human outline. From its shoulders, strange, twisted shapes had been etched into the glass like a pair of mighty wings. Resting nearby was Ignatius's rapier, washed clean of Raven's blood and glittering wetly in the sunlight.

It was then that Jonathan felt it: a huge wave of regret that washed over and through him. It spoke of loss, but also of a refusal to give in and, even more, of hope. Jonathan wasn't aware he was crying until he felt the tears rolling down his cheeks. He touched fingertips to his face in surprise.

"This is the heart of Hobbes End, Jonathan," said Ignatius. "This is where your grandfather fell and where my ancestor Augustus pulled him from the water. One angel, one vicar, one village. Sanctuary."

Jonathan nodded. "I understand," he said. "I can feel Gabriel here. I didn't know how much of himself he gave away." As he stood quietly by the edge of the pond, he sensed something new, something even more extraordinary than Gabriel's regret. It was a voice both powerful and gentle, utterly different from the uncontrolled energy waiting inside him. It was running water, wind in the trees, birds flying, grass growing, and people going about their lives knowing that they had someone to watch over them. It was Hobbes End itself, and it chose that moment to speak to Jonathan.

"Hello," it said.

Jonathan gasped and sank to his knees. It was like someone had lifted an awful weight from his heart, and for the first time since his life had been turned upside down he felt at peace.

"You heard that, didn't you," said Ignatius with a gentle smile.

Jonathan nodded.

"Then perhaps this doesn't end with me," said Ignatius. "Just a thought. Now, if you'll all wait here for a minute."

Jonathan watched as the vicar climbed down into the pond to retrieve his rapier, carefully avoiding the crater left by Gabriel's fall. Sword retrieved, Ignatius scrambled up the muddy bank and shut the sluice gate before rejoining his friends. The pond began to refill, and the outline of the fallen angel disappeared again under a sheet of rippling water.

"Well, there's something you don't see every day," said Grimm.

"Yes," agreed Jonathan. "Now what?"

"Now we wait," said Ignatius. "Now we wait."

Cay sat beside Gabriel, still horrified at the violence that had been visited on the old angel. He reached out a gnarled hand, which Cay grasped and held against her cheek, feeling the bones just beneath the skin.

"I'm old, Cay," said Gabriel. "My time is almost over, but there is one last job to do."

"What do you mean?" asked Cay. "You're still an archangel — you'll live for ages, won't you?"

"Nothing is forever," said Gabriel. "Not Heaven, not Hell, not me. Everything changes. Creation doesn't stand still." He sighed deeply and bowed his head. "I'm sorry you got dragged into all this, Cay. If only you could have seen me before it all fell apart, back when I was Gabriel Artificer. With enough will there was nothing I couldn't build or mend. Through the windows of my wings I used to be able to create worlds. Now I'm but a pale shadow, fit only to build trinkets."

"Don't say that," said Cay.

"I'm sorry, child," said Gabriel. "I don't mean to sound so full of self-pity. There is hope yet."

"So you do think we'll get out of here, then?" said Cay.

"Of course we will; have faith."

"I'll try. I just wish I knew that everyone back home was okay. I hope Jonathan didn't get hurt."

"So do I," said Gabriel.

"It's my eleventh birthday tomorrow," whispered Cay. "The best present I could have would be for us all to be safe and together again, flying kites on the village green."

Gabriel smiled. "That would be a fine birthday present indeed," he said. "I do have something for you, though. I didn't forget."

Cay smiled. "You can give it to me when we get home," she said.

"Yes," said Gabriel, staring blindly out the window. "I think it's a present you won't forget in a hurry."

Chapter 18

REVELATIONS

A midday knock at the vicarage door signaled the arrival of the postman. Ignatius got up to find a brown paper parcel sitting on the doorstep. He picked it up and returned to the kitchen, where Jonathan, with Elgar on his lap, sat waiting. Every minute that ticked by seemed like an hour, and Jonathan felt the calm he had discovered by the pond being rapidly eroded.

"The postie's late today," said Grimm from the pantry. He was rearranging tins of tea in order to keep himself occupied.

"Hmm," nodded Ignatius, fishing a pair of scissors from the cutlery drawer. He had just snipped the string and started to peel open the parcel when the phone in the hall began to ring. They were all expecting it, but it still made them jump.

"Do you think . . . ?" asked Jonathan.

Ignatius nodded, his face impassive. "Something tells me it's not someone trying to sell us insurance. Gather round so you can hear." They all stood next to him as the vicar of Hobbes End lifted the receiver. "This is the Reverend Ignatius Crumb speaking," he said. "Explain yourself, Belial."

"It's a pleasure to finally speak with you, Reverend Crumb," came a deep, mocking voice. "You know who I am, so there's no need for pleasantries."

Jonathan looked at Ignatius in alarm as the vicar scowled and clenched his jaw. "Yes, I've heard of you, Belial. You're a coward, and you disgust me."

"Now now, there's no need for name-calling. I was trying to be civilized."

"Civilized?" blurted Ignatius. "You invade my village, hurt those under my care, and try to steal what isn't yours. In what way is that civilized?"

"*Tch!* Mere semantics." The archdemon chuckled. "Still, I think we can get down to business, don't you?"

"As long as you haven't hurt Jonathan's family or Cay."

"You have my word," lied Belial. "They're here, all

bright-eyed and bushy-tailed. If you do what I ask, then I'll hand them back to you."

"Go on," said Ignatius through gritted teeth.

"I want the boy, and I want Gabriel's clock. I'm going to turn Jonathan into the most feared weapon in all of creation. Gabriel's cherubim that slaughtered us on the plain of Armageddon will be nothing to what Jonathan can become. And when he is ready I will destroy the other archdemons, then destroy Lucifer and be sole ruler in Hell. I know you're listening, Jonathan. Go on, admit it. There's a bit of you that wants this, isn't there? Imagine being greater than Lucifer could ever aspire to be. Just do as I ask and it can all be yours."

The voice inside Jonathan's head began clamoring to be heard. It liked Belial's offer. It wanted a chance to be free, to be able to use such extraordinary power without restraint. Jonathan began to shake until Grimm placed a steadying hand on his shoulder. That was a comfort, but something else made it complete. The village itself. It had accepted him, and it knew that he needed help.

"Be still," it whispered. "Don't be afraid." The shaking subsided, and Jonathan found the strength to listen to Belial without giving in to the fury inside him.

"But now we have an added bonus," the archdemon continued, unable to hide the perverse excitement in his voice. "In his haste to save his grandson, Gabriel has handed me a way to rule not only in Hell but also in Heaven! Imagine that—the armies of Hell marching into an unsuspecting Heaven with Jonathan at their head. Whatever angels are left won't stand a chance. What do you think? Is it worth a shot?"

As Belial laughed down the phone, Ignatius's hand gripped the receiver until his knuckles showed white.

"Well done on defeating Rook and Raven, by the way. Nobody's ever come close before," the archdemon continued. "I'm actually rather impressed. Crow is very upset, though. He's having trouble tying his shoelaces, and I think he'd quite like to return and beat you all to death with his missing arm."

"Oh, please let him try," rumbled Grimm, cracking his knuckles.

"I assume you've figured out how we could trample all over your precious village?" asked Belial.

"Yes," said Ignatius. "Rook and Raven bursting into flames was a helpful hint."

"I'm sure it was. Now to business. I have Darriel, Gabriel, and Miss Forrester safely tucked away. Just so we're clear about what you need to do, if you fail to send me the boy with Gabriel's clock, then your friends will meet with a series of . . . unfortunate events."

"How do I know they're still alive?"

There was a moment's pause before they all heard

Cay's voice. "I'm okay!" she shouted out. A wave of re-lief surged through Jonathan, but then she continued, "And Gabriel's here. He's . . . hurt. He wants to speak with you."

There was a brief pause before Gabriel's voice came on the line. "Ignatius. Say nothing, just listen to me, old friend, since I have little time. There is a door in my workroom that leads to somewhere else. The clock is there, and Jonathan is the only one who can fetch it. Only someone of my bloodline can enter. Tell Jonathan to make sure he takes the watch I gave him, as he'll need it."

"But—" said Ignatius.

"Please!" begged Gabriel. "No questions—just trust me. Everything must change. Tell Jonathan not to be afraid of what will happen when he brings the clock to Belial. Innocence is not so easily lost, Heaven is not so easily destroyed, you—"

"That's enough witless sentiment," snarled Belial. "Now, you have until six o'clock this evening to send me both Jonathan and the clock. If you don't, the conse-quences to your friends will be most unpleasant."

Cay let out a muffled scream, and Jonathan felt sicker than he had believed possible.

"I'll send Crow to escort you," said Belial. "That should give you long enough to fetch Gabriel's masterpiece. Oh, and don't try to fob me off with any old clock, because I know what I'm looking for. Just so you understand who you're dealing with, I sent you a present in the post this morning. What is it my dear mother used to say? Oh, yes, 'It's all fun and games until someone loses an eye!' Best you run along now. Time's a-wasting, tick tock."

The line went dead. Ignatius replaced the handset and turned to look at the parcel on the kitchen table.

"What did he mean?" stammered Jonathan. "What's in it?" He took a step toward the table before Grimm wrapped his arms round him.

"No, lad. Don't look."

With shaking hands Ignatius finished unwrapping the parcel. Being careful that only he could see what was within, he slowly lifted the cardboard lid, and Jonathan watched as all color drained from Ignatius's face. The vicar closed the box, sat at the table, and wept silently, pounding the scarred wood every few seconds with his fist.

Watching the awful pain on Ignatius's gentle face was almost impossible for Jonathan to bear. "What's in the box?" he begged, struggling to release himself from Grimm's grip. "What's Belial done?"

Ignatius got up and stood by Jonathan. Wiping tears of fury from his eyes, he took a deep breath and composed himself. "It doesn't matter," he croaked. "Only what we do next matters."

"But—"

"*No!*" shouted Ignatius. "No *but*s. No *if*s. I know things seem hopeless, but I know your grandfather. He's been standing beside me every day of my life. I *know* him. There's one thing he said to me that I've never forgotten: 'There's no point getting old if you don't get crafty.' He hasn't given in. He has a plan. Now, what do you think we should do?"

Jonathan already knew the answer—he wanted nothing more than to take this fight to Belial, and now he had the chance.

"I'm going to go fetch Gabriel's clock," he said. "And when I meet Belial I'm going to shove it down his throat!"

"Attaboy," chortled Grimm. "As soon as I fix her, Isobel will have an appointment with Belial that that demon really isn't going to like!" Grinning so widely, it looked as though his head might split, he gave a practice swing with an imaginary cricket bat.

Elgar jumped onto Grimm's shoulders. "I second that statement. I'll bite him on the bum so hard, he'll never be able to sit down again!"

Then something occurred to Jonathan. "What did

Gabriel mean when he said I'd need the watch he gave to me?"

"I'm not sure," said Ignatius. "But Gabriel wouldn't have mentioned it unless it was important. Regardless, it means that something of your grandfather's is always with you, and that's a good thing."

"Yes," said Jonathan. "It's a good thing."

"We're going along too, and that's final," said Montgomery. "Aren't we, Mr. Stubbs?"

"Hell, yes! I've missed one fight, and I'm not passing up the chance to find myself another. Gargoyle honor is at stake!"

Ignatius sighed, but he couldn't help a smile. "Okay then, boys, down you come. You're nowhere near recharged yet, but I'm not going to stop you if this is what you want to do."

"But what if you can't get through this door of Gabriel's?" asked Jonathan as Montgomery and Stubbs landed on the drive in front of him. "He said that only someone of his bloodline could enter."

"He helped make us, and we're not actually alive," said Montgomery. "So we're going to give it a shot."

"Yeah," said Stubbs. "If we can't go with you, then we'll sulk for England, but at least we tried."

"What he said," agreed Montgomery.

Elgar sat by Jonathan's legs, unusually quiet.

"What's up?" asked Jonathan.

"If I'm not there to keep you out of trouble, then who knows what'll happen! I'm just annoyed that I can't go with you, that's all."

"I know, cat," said Jonathan. "Come on, let's get to Gabriel's cottage. The sooner I fetch the clock, the sooner we can stop Belial. It's time I took the fight to him!"

Chapter 19

WAITING FOR THE CAVALRY

C ay sat on the bed and thought about her parents. It was easier to think of them at home worried about her than it was to think about the danger she and Gabriel were in. And she knew Belial wasn't joking. If someone didn't arrive with the clock, then she and Gabriel were dead meat. Or, more accurately, several neatly wrapped boxes of dead meat. The thought made her shudder as the minutes ticked by.

Gabriel still sat in a chair by the window, staring sightlessly at the afternoon sky. Cay was saddened to see how frail he looked, the bandages wrapped around his head only increasing his apparent helplessness.

"Will you be strong enough to fight Belial?" she asked.

"I don't know," he replied.

"Oh," said Cay, hugging her hands to her chest.

"Does that worry you?" asked Gabriel.

"Yes, it does!" said Cay. "How can you stop him when you're . . ."

"Broken? Appearances can be deceptive, Cay."

"I hope so," she said. "Or we've had it!"

Gabriel laughed. As Cay watched, some of the weariness fell away from his face. She had no idea how the old angel could be so sure of himself, but she hoped he was right. She walked over to him and squeezed his shoulder.

"Do you know what my favorite thing in the whole world is?" he asked her.

She shook her head.

"Flying. To slip the surly bonds of earth and dance the skies on laughter-silvered wings. I haven't been able to fly since my fall. I chose to create Hobbes End, and in giving away so much power I knew that I'd never fly again. I'll never regret that decision, but sometimes . . ."

A thought occurred to Cay. "What will happen when Jonathan brings your clock to Belial in exchange for us? He'll have everything he wants, and then he'll kill us anyway."

"Possibly," said Gabriel, a curious look on his face. "But you never know. The cavalry may ride in to save us at the last minute. Do you know what a deus ex machina is, Cay?"

She shook her head.

"It's Latin. It's when, against all logic, some divine intervention or miraculous happening saves the day. It literally means 'god from a machine.'"

"Is that what we're hoping for? A miracle?"

Gabriel smiled. "Funny things, miracles," he said. "Sometimes they actually happen."

"That's not very reassuring," she said.

"No, I suppose it isn't," he replied. "Have faith, Cay."

With a sigh of frustration she leaned against the windowsill. In silence she kept Gabriel company as she watched the sun pass its zenith and begin its slow journey toward the horizon. The shadows lengthened, and Cay prayed that Gabriel's optimism wasn't just wishful thinking.

Chapter 20

HERE THERE BE DRAGONS

Jonathan stood amid the broken glass and scattered books in Gabriel's workroom. Behind him, Ignatius and Grimm waited quietly. Jonathan was glad they were there; he just hoped that he wouldn't let them down. So much hinged on what he did next.

"Where's this door, then?" asked Elgar.

"How about this?" said Stubbs, walking over to the gable wall where a plain wooden door with a brass doorknob lay flush with the brick. He rapped on it with his knuckles. There was a hollow, booming sound. "Perhaps it's a wardrobe?"

"Yeah, and we all know what happens to children who go ferreting around in magical wardrobes, don't we?" said Elgar, jumping onto the workbench. "They grow up in some faraway land, accidentally find their way back home, realize they're only twelve again, and spend the next two years in therapy."

Jonathan laughed despite himself.

The cat nodded toward the door. "Do you think that's what Gabriel was talking about?"

Jonathan looked around the room. The walls were covered with racks of clock parts and boxes of junk, but there was no other door that he could see. "I guess it's a good place to start," he said, shrugging his shoulders.

"Ah, the optimism of youth," said the cat. "I'm laying odds that all you'll find when you open that door is a couple of brooms, a foot of brickwork, and a two-meter drop into the churchyard."

"Okay, then," said Jonathan. He strode forward, turned the doorknob, and pulled.

Bright light flooded into the attic, and everyone gasped. It was difficult to see clearly, but through the door Jonathan thought he could see a huge swath of white sand.

"Me first," said Stubbs, bounding through the door before anyone could stop him.

Montgomery put his hands over his eyes. "Are you dead?" he shouted to his friend.

"Nah," said Stubbs. "You really need to come have a look at this!"

"How's it possible?" Jonathan gasped, still staring through the doorway.

"There's no way you're doing this without me," said Elgar. "I don't care what Gabriel said about bloodlines."

"I think—" said Montgomery, raising a cautionary finger, but he was too late to stop the cat from taking a run at the doorway.

The moment Elgar's nose drew level with the door frame, it was as if the cat had been plugged in to an electric socket. His fur stood on end, his tail went rigid, and he let out a screech of pain as he was sent flying back across the workshop to land in a box of wood shavings.

Jonathan ran over and picked up the shivering cat. "Are you all right, Elgar?" he asked.

The cat looked at him with wide, scared eyes. "That was not fun," he croaked. "You know that feeling you get when you lick a flashlight battery?"

Jonathan shook his head.

"Well, if you did, what just happened to me was about a zillion times worse!"

"I tried to warn you," said Montgomery.

Elgar sighed and drooped his whiskers.

"Grimm and I are going to stay right here until Jonathan comes back," said Ignatius. "Why don't you wait with us?"

"Because I want to go with him!" shouted Elgar. "Think of something, Monty."

The gargoyle scratched his chin. "Perhaps if you carried Elgar?" he said to Jonathan.

"It's worth a go. You up for it?" Jonathan asked the cat.

"Well, if it happens again, then at least I get the satisfaction of landing on you," said Elgar.

"Thanks for the support," said Jonathan. He took a firm hold of Elgar. "Right, let's do this." He turned to look at Ignatius and Grimm. "I'll be back before you know it," he said.

They smiled at him.

Shutting his eyes, Jonathan put out his hand and took a tentative step forward. The second his fingers drew level with the door frame it was as if they'd suddenly been pushed into a vat of really thick, electrified syrup. Jonathan could feel the gate's resistance to Elgar. It knew the cat wasn't of Gabriel's bloodline, and it didn't really want to let him through. Taking a deep breath, Jonathan slowly and calmly reached for what he knew lay inside him. He wasn't angry or afraid, he wasn't facing a monster, but he focused on how he just wanted his friend by his side. Amazingly, he felt the gate obey. All resistance evaporated, and with Elgar and Montgomery he stepped forward into a dream.

There were stars, so many stars all close together. Their light was so bright, it hurt his eyes.

"Blimey!" said Montgomery. "Will you look at that!"

Jonathan was simply staring in awe at his surroundings. He stood on a vast, circular plain of rolling sand. High above, a shimmering dome of pale energy was all that separated him from an infinite black void dotted with countless pinpricks of silver light. Inside the dome flowed the same never-ending stream of mathematical symbols and equations that he'd seen inside his wings. He turned round and caught one last glimpse of Ignatius's worried face before the door closed. It was so odd just seeing the door there, resting on the sand without anything to support it.

"Where are we?" he whispered.

"Temporary quantum dream-state singularity," said Stubbs confidently.

"How on earth do you know that?" asked Elgar, jumping to the ground. "And what does it *mean?*"

"Oh, Gabriel used to come talk to us about stuff when he was thinking up new things to build. I've got no idea what any of it actually meant, but it sounded very interesting."

Jonathan shook his head, astonished at the power required to create something so extraordinary. *Could I build something like this?* he wondered. And then he saw it, far away across the sand, rising like a sword to the heavens—a massive, impossibly delicate tower of white stone, its base surrounded by a ring of flying buttresses.

"There," he said, feeling a tug from deep inside. "That's where we have to go."

"Are you sure?" asked Elgar.

"I'm sure." Jonathan nodded; he could feel something calling to him, faintly, like a distant heartbeat. He checked his watch. "Look, it's gone one o'clock. We've got less than five hours until we meet with Crow, so let's hurry."

They set off toward the tower. The quiet was absolute; there was no wind, no movement, no life of any sort. Overhead the stars wheeled through space, a constant reminder to Jonathan that time was passing, and he knew the price for failure, so every minute that ticked by pressed down upon him.

After an hour of walking, he began to see strange shapes poking up through the sand—angular pieces of metal glinting in the starlight. Some of the shapes looked strangely familiar.

"That looks like the head of a Tyrannosaurus Rex," he said, pointing to where an enormous metal skull lay half buried. One uncovered eye socket stared blindly upward, and half its teeth were missing. A few feet away a giant claw looked like it was trying to dig its way out of a sandy grave.

"Here there be dragons," whispered Montgomery.

"What do you mean?" asked Jonathan, a shiver suddenly running down his spine.

"It's something Gabriel used to say when he wanted us to stop poking our noses into things. I always thought he was joking."

"But what is it?" asked Jonathan. "And look, there are more of them."

The nearer they got to the tower, the more skeletons they found. Some were just scraps of metal; others were almost complete, lying exposed on the sand as if asleep. They were so big that when one blocked their path, Jonathan was able to walk straight between the ribs and out the other side.

"What was Gabriel doing here?" asked Elgar.

"I don't know," said Jonathan. "But we don't have time to think about it. We need to get inside that tower. The nearer we get to it, the stronger it gets."

"The stronger what gets?"

"I can't explain it," said Jonathan. "It's like something's calling me."

Trying to ignore the dead stares of the skeletons littered about them, he urged himself onward until he reached the base of the tower. It was then he realized that something was very wrong.

From far away the tower had looked impossibly perfect. Up close it was anything but. The structure was riven with cracks and jagged holes, and the sand beneath littered with debris. Between two crumbling buttresses, an archway led inside.

"It's falling apart," said Jonathan. "Why?"

There was a sudden crackling from high above. He looked up and saw the energy dome flicker. As the formulae within it twisted and changed, grew jagged, the ground shook and Jonathan put out his arms to steady himself.

"Look out!" cried Stubbs.

Jonathan just had time to see what was falling toward him when Stubbs slammed into his back, sending him sprawling. A stone block the size of a door crashed into the sand where he had been standing, right on top of the little gargoyle.

"No!" shouted Montgomery, a horrified look on his face as he desperately pushed at the block. Jonathan staggered to his feet and joined Montgomery, but it was no use—the stone wouldn't budge. They stepped back and stared at each other, disbelief written on their faces. "He can't just be gone like that, can he?" asked Montgomery.

"I . . . I . . ." stammered Jonathan, not knowing what to say.

"Can't you use your wings to move it?" suggested Elgar.

"Maybe," said Jonathan, but then something stopped him. He looked up at the energy dome. It had steadied, but now and again it flickered like a guttering candle. Small aftershocks vibrated the sand at their feet, and the tower behind them groaned. "I think this place is collapsing, Monty," he said. "If I can't control my wings, then I crack that dome like an eggshell. I don't know what might happen after that, but it couldn't be good."

"Oh." The gargoyle sighed.

"Why is it collapsing?" asked Elgar.

Jonathan felt a sinking feeling in the pit of his stomach as he understood what was happening. "It was built by Gabriel. It's powered by Gabriel. If it's collapsing, that means . . ."

"Means what?" asked Elgar.

"It means we have to hurry," said Jonathan. "It means my grandfather is getting weaker. I need to rescue him, and Dad and Cay. We have to keep going."

"But we can't just leave him . . ." begged Montgomery.

Jonathan felt awful. He had an overwhelming need

to find the clock, to get home, to bring everything to its end. But to leave the little gargoyle behind? This was Stubbs. Brave, unhinged Stubbs, who had pummeled Raven in the face and saved Cay and her dad; this was the gargoyle who had just saved him. Abandoning Stubbs was not an option.

"I don't know what to do," he said to Elgar.

"I think you—" The cat stopped speaking and shot into the air with a howl. "It's those skeleton things!" he cried, hiding behind Jonathan. "One of them just tried to grab me."

Jonathan looked at where Elgar had been sitting and saw the sand sinking downward in a funnel shape. Something pointed rose up from it—a stone ear clutched in a stone paw.

Stubbs clawed his way into the light, coughing and spluttering. From the expression on his face it was obvious he was particularly annoyed. "Look at this!" he said, pointing to his broken ear. "Look at it. One hundred and thirty years without a scratch, and now it decides to fall off."

"Mr. Stubbs!" cried Montgomery happily.

"You saved my life, Stubbsey," said Jonathan, kneeling down to pat the gargoyle on the shoulder. "Thank you."

"S'all right." Stubbs shrugged. "Look after this, will you?" he said, giving Jonathan his broken ear. "We can fix it later. Right, where were we?"

Smiling at the sheer indestructibility of the gargoyle, Jonathan got to his feet and turned to face the archway that led inside the tower. "Let's go," he said.

They walked into the cool, dim interior. It took Jonathan's eyes a while to adjust from the glare outside, but when they did his heart sank even further. All around him was evidence of grinding decay. Starlight poured into the cavernous interior of the tower through holes in the ceiling, and more blocks of stone littered the floor. The silence and desolation were absolute. All Jonathan could hear was the sound of his own labored breathing and the gentle crunch of sand beneath his feet.

"Where are you?" Jonathan whispered as he peered into the gloom. And then he saw it, something glowing on what looked like an altar on the far side of the tower. Something that sang to him. He ran forward until he could see it clearly.

Floating just above the carved stone surface of the altar was a glass sphere the size of a goldfish bowl. It pulsed with muted bursts of multicolored light, and inside it a mechanism of mind-boggling complexity ticked quietly.

"That's it," said Jonathan. "That's Gabriel's clock! That's the back-door key to Heaven."

"My whiskers agree with you," said Elgar, his eyes narrowing in thought. "But would Gabriel have just left it sitting there?"

"I don't care!" shouted Jonathan. "Let's just grab it and get out of here." He took another step forward.

A rumbling began to echo around the empty shell of the tower. Dislodged by the vibration, trickles of sand sifted down from the ceiling high above. A long, torturous screech of metal on stone assaulted their ears, and from out of the darkness behind the altar a terrifying shape uncoiled itself. With whiplike speed the sinuous body of an enormous dragon rose up and lunged forward, slamming its forelegs protectively to the ground in front of the clock. The floor heaved as claws tore into the stone, sparks flying in all directions. Knocked off balance, Jonathan toppled backwards to land in a heap between Elgar and the gargoyles.

The flaming blue eyes of the dragon fixed upon him as he huddled, shaking, between his friends. Rearing up, it thrust its head forward, opened its jaws, and roared like thunder.

Utterly terrified, Jonathan sat frozen to the spot.

"I think I know what those skeletons outside in the sand were for," said Montgomery with a squeak.

"What?" whispered Jonathan.

"Practice for creating that!"

Jonathan felt the voice begin to call from inside him again. He shut his eyes and willed his wings not to appear. If he let them out, they'd split this pocket universe of Gabriel's wide open, probably killing them all. Then again, this dragon would probably kill them anyway.

He opened his eyes and forced himself to be calm. The dragon hadn't moved. It just sat between them and the clock, its huge head swaying gently. The seconds ticked by, and, swallowing hard, a dry-mouthed Jonathan slowly got to his feet. The dragon snorted and shifted its bulk but made no move to attack.

"Why aren't we all in mangled pieces?" mewled Elgar.

"Why would my grandfather just send us here to be eaten?" said Jonathan. "This dragon is guarding the clock; we just have to figure out how to get past it."

Trying to stop his heart from beating its way out of his chest, he moved closer until he came eye to eye with the dragon. It shifted position again, and as it did so the shafts of starlight that pierced the ruined tower played over the massive body like so many torches. The scales that covered the dragon were actually thousands of overlapping metal plates, held in place with tiny rivets. Where the starlight brushed them the plates shone a deep burnished silver.

Jonathan looked up and saw two vast wings, outstretched and gleaming. The delicacy of their construction was extraordinary—flexible metal panels hammered so thin, they were almost translucent, held in place by a complex framework of struts and pins. The creature was a work of art. And there on the dragon's chest was a polished metal plaque with the word BRASS engraved on it, followed by a small capital G.

"So you're Brass," Jonathan whispered in astonishment. The dragon snorted, and Jonathan assumed this meant yes. "And Gabriel built you and asked you to guard the clock?"

Another snort.

"Gabriel is my grandfather," said Jonathan. "He's a prisoner of the archdemon Belial, and he sent me here to fetch the clock. I have to take it to Gabriel or Belial will kill him, my father, and my friend Cay."

Brass snorted again, and Jonathan took a step toward the altar. The dragon's jaws slammed shut just in front of Jonathan's face, taking the skin off the end of his nose.

"Ahhhhhh!" he screamed, dropping to his knees in terror.

There was a blur of motion and an almighty *clang*

as Stubbs flew past Jonathan and thumped the dragon right on the end of his snout. *"Bad Brass!"* shouted Stubbs. *"Naughty Brass!"*

"We are going to die," said Elgar, putting his paws over his eyes.

Rather than flying into a rage and tearing them all apart, Brass seemed rather taken aback. It retreated from the furious Stubbs, but the bass rumble in its chest made it very clear that anyone who made a grab for the clock was going to get eaten.

Montgomery helped a shaking Jonathan to his feet. "Why did it do that?" he asked the gargoyle.

"I don't know," said Montgomery. "And it's not an *it*, it's a *she*. She's a construct, just like me and Stubbs."

"How do you know it's a she?" asked Elgar.

"I just do, okay!" replied Montgomery. "It's a construct thing."

Jonathan looked at the watch on his wrist. It was after three. Almost half their time was gone. He racked his brain. How to get Brass to let them take the clock before it was too late?

It was then Jonathan had an idea. He undid Gabriel's watch from his wrist and held it up for Brass to see. The dragon sniffed it and shifted to one side, but she still seemed reluctant to let Jonathan past. It was as if she wanted to but couldn't until something else happened.

A stray shaft of starlight clipped the watch as it dangled in the air, and Jonathan realized he'd had the answer all along. It was engraved on the watch's back plate.

"Deus ex machina!" he shouted.

Brass uncoiled herself from the altar and stood aside. It almost looked like she was smiling.

"Hurrah!" said Montgomery, high-fiving Stubbs with a *donk* sound.

Jonathan slowly walked forward, but Brass gave no indication that she would interfere. He sighed with relief. "I knew Gabriel was trying to tell me something when he said I'd need the watch. He wanted to make sure I brought it with me."

In front of him, the crystal globe of Gabriel's clock hung in the air waiting to be picked up. It sounded like it was singing to itself. Jonathan reached out with shaking hands and pulled the clock toward him, hugging it to his chest.

"Phew!" said Elgar. "Right, how do we get home?"

"I guess we have to get back to where we came in," said Jonathan. "We need to get a move on; we don't have much time left."

They turned to leave, but Montgomery stayed where he was. "What about Brass?" he said. "We can't just leave her here. She'll be all lonely."

Jonathan could see the dragon's eyes blazing in the

darkness. "That's a good point, Monty. Brass, would you like to—"

Before Jonathan could say anything else, an awful rending sound echoed through the tower. Chunks of stone rained down as the ground heaved and bucked, sending them sprawling. Jonathan held the clock tightly to his chest so it wouldn't fall and break.

"Oh, now what?" howled Elgar.

Stubbs picked himself up and ran to the tower entrance. "Oh dear," he said, pointing to the sky. "That's not good, is it?"

Jonathan ran after him and looked up to see myriad rips appear in the energy dome. This time they didn't steady and close. They began to widen. Beneath them, twisting columns of sand shot upward and began venting into space. Air whistled past Jonathan's head, and the tower let out a tortured shriek.

"We're too late!" gasped Jonathan. "The dome's collapsing; we'll never get back to the door before this place rips itself apart."

A snort from behind him made Jonathan turn. Brass barged past and craned her neck to look at the chaos high above; nestled in the hollow between her enormous shoulders crouched Montgomery and Elgar.

"I think she wants to give us a lift," the cat said, grinning.

Jonathan stared in astonishment as the dragon used one of her claws to scoop him and Stubbs up before dropping them onto her back.

"I don't think she can fly," Montgomery shouted, "but I bet she can run!"

Jonathan was about to agree when an explosion ripped through the air beside him, closely followed by another and then another. Stone shards pinged off Brass's hide as the flying buttresses that supported the tower finally gave way.

"Giddyup!" cried Elgar.

Brass looked at the cat with a raised eyebrow but did as she was asked. With a lurch that almost unseated Jonathan, the dragon launched herself forward like a shell from a howitzer. With one arm holding on to the clock and the other gripping the scales on Brass's back, Jonathan could only stare, wide-eyed, as the dragon thundered into the maelstrom of sand and howling wind.

From behind them, an impossibly tall shadow threw itself along their path.

"Brass, the tower!" cried Jonathan. "It's falling toward us!"

The dragon snorted, glanced over her shoulder, and increased her speed. She may as well have been flying, as her feet didn't seem to touch the ground.

Jonathan didn't dare look at the destruction that followed them. He knew it was pointless; he just prayed they could find the door before they were either flattened or sucked into space. The ground shook, and all around them tornadoes of sand spiraled upward.

"Where's the door?" he shouted.

"There!" bellowed Montgomery, clinging to one of Brass's ears and pointing ahead of them. The dragon dipped her nose and gave one last burst of speed as Jonathan finally saw the exit. As they drew near, the door banged open to reveal the startled faces of Ignatius and Grimm. The two men took one look at what was thundering toward them and fled from Gabriel's workroom as fast as they could.

Unable to stop himself, Jonathan cast one last look over his shoulder. Directly above him, the pinnacle of the tower hung in the air, its incredible weight only seconds away from grinding them all to pulp.

"We're not going to fit!" yowled Elgar.

"I don't think Brass cares," Stubbs shouted back.

Without breaking stride, the dragon wrapped her wings over her body, covering everyone who clung to her back. Trying to make herself as small as possible, she hit the doorway at full speed just as the tower finally crashed to the ground.

For a moment, all was darkness and choking brick

dust. Jonathan couldn't see anything, but against his chest he cradled Gabriel's clock, and right now that was all that mattered.

There was a rumbling of masonry, and the bright sunlight of a summer afternoon made him blink. He looked up and saw two huge wings unfold into the air of Hobbes End, scattering bricks, wood, and thatch in all directions. Behind him, Brass snorted and shook dust from her head. The dragon had shielded them from the cottage's destruction.

An amazed Ignatius appeared in front of him and reached down to help Jonathan up.

"Now that is what I call an entrance!" He grinned. Then he saw what Jonathan was cradling in his arms, and his eyes widened in relief and astonishment.

"You, my boy," he said, "are a credit to your grandfather."

At Jonathan's feet, Elgar and the gargoyles dusted themselves off and gazed skyward.

"And where do you propose that *she* stay?" asked Elgar, waving a paw at Brass.

"I have absolutely no idea," said Ignatius, shaking his head.

From around the corner of the church the inhabitants of Hobbes End ran toward the wreckage of Gabriel's cottage. Given that they were greeted by the sight of a massive mechanical dragon towering above them, they all took it rather well.

Mr. Flynn walked up to them, his arm linked with that of his wife. He glanced up at Brass and smiled. "Hello, young man," he said to Jonathan. "Would your new friend like a sherbet lemon?"

Chapter 21

A Glimmer of Hope

Trapped in her well-appointed prison, Cay lay on the bed and watched Gabriel as he stared into space. He looked gray, and his body was shaking with effort. It was as if he was concentrating on something to the exclusion of all else, something that was taking all his remaining strength to control.

With a sudden gasp Gabriel stood up and leaned against the window, arms outstretched and palms flat against the glass. Sweat ran down his face to soak into the bandages that wrapped his ruined eyes. He drew a ragged breath.

"Well done, grandson," he said, slumping back into his chair. The room filled with the scent of apples and beeswax, and Cay watched as Gabriel visibly relaxed.

A look of serenity settled over him, and he gave her an exhausted smile. "Jonathan's found the clock," he said to Cay. "For a minute there I didn't think I had the strength to keep my hiding place intact."

Cay's heart leaped in her chest, and she sprang from the bed to stand by Gabriel. Whatever he'd been doing had cost him dearly; he'd shrunk into himself somehow, become less than he was.

"That's brilliant!" she said. "But what about you? You look so tired."

"I haven't left Hobbes End in over three hundred years," he said. "The farther I'm away from it, the weaker I become and the more difficult it is to maintain that which I've built. I had to give Jonathan time to fetch the clock from where I'd hidden it, but . . . it was hard."

"Will you be all right?" asked Cay, kneeling beside the angel and squeezing his hand.

Gabriel nodded. "I will now," he said. "My grandson is coming, and Belial will pay the price for what he has done. Together Jonathan and I will teach that archdemon what it is to be afraid."

Chapter 22

MEANWHILE, BACK AT THE VICARAGE ...

Is Brass going to be all right?" asked Jonathan as he stood by Grimm's Daimler.

"I think so," said Grimm. "She seems to be sleeping happily in what's left of Gabriel's cottage. As long as Professor Morgenstern doesn't keep prodding Brass to find out how she works, then I think everything should be okay. Ignatius, we've got ten minutes to make our rendezvous!"

Jonathan watched as the vicar of Hobbes End helped the obviously tired gargoyles back onto their gateposts.

"You've done the family proud, boys," said the vicar, patting them fondly on their heads. They beamed with pleasure at having been of use and gave Ignatius crisp salutes.

"Ta very much," said Stubbs.

"Yes, thanks awfully," agreed Montgomery.

"You two need some rest," said Ignatius. "You've earned it. Oh, and Mr. Stubbs?"

"Yes?"

"We'll find a way to fix your ear. Don't worry."

Stubbs grinned happily, and the gargoyles settled into position, stretched, and yawned.

"We had an adventure, didn't we, Mr. Stubbs?" said Montgomery to his friend.

"Indeed we did, Mr. Montgomery," replied Stubbs. "Indeed we did."

Within seconds they were both fast asleep and snoring like foghorns.

Ignatius joined everyone in the Daimler but stuck his head out the window to say goodbye to Angus McFadden and the rest of the villagers who stood with him.

"We'll be back soon," he said, meaning every word.

"Aye," said Angus. "We have a wee beastie to keep an eye on things while you're gone. Give that archdemon a proper Hobbes End welcome, won't ye?"

"Count on it," said Ignatius.

"Ready?" asked Grimm.

"Ready," said Ignatius. He looked at the bowler hat that Grimm was wearing. "Was that Rook's?" he asked.

"Yep," said Grimm. "What do you think?"

Ignatius pondered for a moment. "Suits you," he replied.

Grimm beamed happily and started the engine.

Ignatius turned to look at the passengers in the back seat. "Everyone okay with what we're about to do?"

Mr. Forrester nodded. "Joanne's upset that she's too unwell to come with us. She said that if I don't come back with our daughter, and with both of us in one piece, she's going to kill me!"

Ignatius grinned at him.

"I'm ready," said Jonathan, sitting next to Elgar with the clock on his lap.

"You know my opinion," said the cat. "Follow me, lads — I'm right behind you!"

"Good," said Ignatius. He turned to Grimm. "Let's get cracking, shall we? Our escort should be outside the forest entrance."

"My pleasure," said Grimm.

As Belial had promised, they found Crow waiting for them in the black Rolls-Royce. Without ceremony the car sped away, Crow somehow managing to drive with only his left hand, leaving Grimm to follow at a distance. As they drove off, Jonathan stared at the clock in his lap. It was still humming and giving off pulses of light. Oddly, Jonathan realized that he wasn't scared. Just the opposite, in fact. The nearer they got to the monster that had torn his life apart, the more angry he became. There was only one thing he was really afraid of, and that was being overwhelmed by the power inside him. He remembered what his grandfather had said to him when they'd talked in the church.

What happens if I can't control it?

Then you turn into another Lucifer, and you end up destroying that which you profess to love.

The thought that he might hurt someone he cared about, if he attacked Belial, scared him more than the thought of facing the archdemon himself.

The two cars plowed on through country lanes for some time, dusk fell, and Grimm switched on the Daimler's headlights. Occasionally they passed other vehicles, but as night fell even they ceased.

Their journey ended suddenly as the Rolls-Royce slowed before turning left into a wide driveway. As the Daimler pulled in behind it, Jonathan could see a pair of huge wrought-iron gates hung from stone gateposts.

"Come into my parlor, said the spider to the fly," mumbled Elgar as he peered out the car window.

"That's not very cheery," said Grimm.

"But what the spider doesn't know," Elgar continued, "is that the fly is really spoiling for a fight and has a cricket bat tucked down the back of its trousers!"

"Did you manage to fix Isobel, then?" asked Jonathan.

"Oh, yes," said Grimm. "It's amazing what you can do with some wood glue and a vice. Isobel is in the trunk and just waiting to be introduced to Belial."

The Daimler drove on as the gates swung shut behind them.

They were now on enemy territory.

Chapter 23

BETTER THE DEVIL YOU KNOW

Belial stared at the approaching cars through an upstairs window, his eyes blazing with unnatural hunger. Allowing himself a death's-head smile, he turned away from the window and made his way to the large, elegantly decorated ballroom at the rear of the mansion. At the far end, before a huge picture window, two heavy wooden chairs had been placed on the floor. The one to the left was occupied by Cay, and the one to the right by Gabriel. They were both tied securely with lengths of rope.

Cay shrank from Belial as he walked to stand between the two chairs; the awful smell that surrounded the archdemon was so strong, she had difficulty keeping her stomach under control. Gabriel sat quietly in his chair, but he turned to Cay and smiled reassuringly. "Whatever happens, do not fear," he whispered.

The large double doors set into the far wall banged open, and the one-armed Crow ushered the visitors from Hobbes End inside. Alert and unafraid, Jonathan walked in between Ignatius and Grimm. They strode forward until Crow blocked their path, hissing at them with a wide-open mouth full of jagged teeth. Jonathan glared at the demon with utter contempt while Ignatius stopped and tucked his pipe into the corner of his mouth.

Grimm leaned forward and smiled menacingly at Crow. "Just one hat to go," he said, pointing Isobel at the demon's head. "Just the one."

Crow winced but refused to budge.

A growl from Kenneth Forrester signaled that he'd seen his daughter where she sat tied to her chair.

"It's all right, Dad!" shouted Cay. "It's going to be all right!"

Jonathan smiled at Cay, but when he turned and saw the blood-encrusted bandage round his grandfather's face, he knew what had been in the box that Belial had sent to them that morning. The simmering rage that had been building inside him was just seconds from tearing its way free when Gabriel gently shook his head. For a moment Jonathan didn't think he could stop it, but by shutting his eyes and swallowing hard he some-how managed to avoid giving in to that awful voice that urged him to destroy.

Clutching the clock so tightly, his knuckles turned white, Jonathan turned his attention to Belial. He was just as Elgar had described—a tall, thin, shambling corpse of a man.

"Welcome," said Belial. "Crow, please stop frighten-ing our guests."

Keeping a close eye on Grimm, the demon backed away.

Staring impassively at Belial, Ignatius sucked hard on the stem of his pipe. "You don't look at all well," he said. "Perhaps your past sins are catching up with you?"

"Perhaps they are!" said Belial, a febrile light in his eyes. "The clock, if you please?" He held out his hand.

Jonathan looked to his grandfather for guidance.

"Give him the clock," said Gabriel, somehow know-ing what was in Jonathan's heart. "Don't be afraid."

Jonathan stayed where he was, uncertainty filling him. *I'm giving Belial exactly what he wants,* he thought.

"Come, my little general," said Belial, holding his arms wide in a hideous mockery of reassurance. "Let me show you the freedom of absolute power."

Jonathan looked at Ignatius. The vicar's face radiated loathing for the monster that stood in front of them, but he placed a gentle hand on Jonathan's shoulder. "We are here with you," he said. "You are not alone. Be strong. Do as your grandfather asks."

Jonathan took a deep breath and turned to face Belial. It was only the knowledge that he might kill everyone if he summoned his wings that stopped him from wiping that smug rictus of a smile from the archdemon's rotting face. Dredging up every ounce of self-control he had, Jonathan stepped forward, his boots clumping loudly on the wooden floor.

"Kneel before me, boy," Belial demanded.

Swallowing hard and trying to ignore the stench of decay that oozed from Belial, Jonathan sank slowly to his knees. The voice inside him was screaming now: "How dare you prostrate yourself? This is the thing that has destroyed your life, hurt your family and your friends. Why not just tear it apart? How can you kneel before it? *It is not your equal!*"

Belial reached out, but instead of taking the clock, he placed his hands on either side of Jonathan's head. Jonathan's body seized as if he was having a fit — every nerve sang with pain, and every muscle fiber went rigid as Belial reached for the power where it raged impotently inside him.

The voice was suddenly silenced, and Jonathan was filled with an awful, cold emptiness. He slumped twitching to the floor, and Belial gently lifted the clock from his numb arms.

The archdemon bent his head to whisper in Jonathan's ear. "You are mine now, little general. For the time being I have clipped your wings. You will do nothing unless I give you permission. You will obey me if you want to avoid your father's fate. I tore off his wings piece by piece until he told me where you were. Then I dumped his body at Heaven's gate. If he still lives, I'm sure he'll be suitably dismayed to see an army marching to destroy him with his son at its head."

Despite struggling as hard as possible, Jonathan found he couldn't move. His body refused to obey him, and his mind was just a reeling mass of pain. Every breath he took felt like he was inhaling broken glass. He couldn't even close his eyes as tears ran down his face. Belial had him completely under his control.

Dad, he mouthed, but no sound came out.

"WHAT HAVE YOU DONE?" bellowed Grimm. He wasn't shouting at Belial, but at Gabriel.

The big man was about to launch himself toward the archdemon, but Ignatius grabbed his arm. "No, Halcyon. Please. Have faith."

"*Faith in what?* I promised Jonathan I wouldn't let Belial have him, and yet that's exactly what we've just done. Do something, Gabriel!"

"Yes, old man," chuckled Belial, gazing lovingly at the clock in his hands. "Why don't you *do* something?"

"You have what you wanted," said the angel. "You have my grandson and the key to Heaven itself. Let Cay go."

"Very well. Since I'm feeling all magnanimous in victory . . . Crow, let her father free the girl."

The second her bonds were untied, Cay leaped into her father's arms, sobbing with relief as she hugged him. "Jonathan," she cried, turning to stare at her friend where he lay pale and still on the floor.

"Untie the angel as well, human," said Belial. "Let's have some fun seeing if he can put up any kind of a fight."

The ropes that bound him fell away, and Gabriel got stiffly to his feet. He shuffled blindly toward the sound of Belial's voice.

"Now, old man," said Belial. "Why don't you show me what an archangel can do? You won't be able to summon help, of course. Even if you had the strength, your brother Raphael doesn't seem to care much for anything outside Heaven anymore. In fact, rumor has it that your brother has gone quite, quite mad."

"I know," said Gabriel, his voice immeasurably sad.

"Once I rule in Hell," taunted Belial, "I'm going to use this clock of yours to destroy your brother and capture Heaven. In his current condition, Raphael may even consider it a mercy. The best bit is that there's nothing you can do to stop it!"

Gabriel lowered his head, and Ignatius felt like weeping for him. Had all their struggling come to this? Humiliation and despair? Then the angel raised his head once more, and Ignatius couldn't believe his eyes. Instead of being racked with sorrow, Gabriel was smiling.

"I think you may be disappointed," said the angel.

Belial blinked in consternation. "What do you—?"

"I'm Gabriel Artificer, and as I often say to Ignatius, there's no point getting old if you don't get crafty!"

Belial choked out an incredulous laugh. "I have your clock. With this I can—"

"DO ABSOLUTELY NOTHING!" roared the angel. "It's beautiful, isn't it? It's a miracle of engineering fit to grace the bedside tables of kings, of queens." He paused and turned to Cay where she sat huddled with her father. "Or even the bedside table of a brave young woman who wanted something special for her birthday."

Cay gaped in astonishment. "You mean . . . ?"

"I mean that Rook made an assumption, and he got it wrong," said Gabriel. He turned back to Belial. "Just because something looks like it should be the back-door key to Heaven doesn't mean that it is. Perhaps it's simply a beautiful present for a friend. You've got the wrong clock, Belial; the real one is somewhere else entirely. Happy birthday, Cay!" Gabriel clicked his fingers, and the sphere in Belial's hands went dark and silent.

The archdemon glared at him. Opening his hands, he dropped the lifeless clock to the floor, and it struck the wooden parquet and exploded, shards of glass and delicate components flying in all directions.

Before Ignatius realized what was happening, before Grimm could raise Isobel, Belial reached out, placed his hands on either side of Gabriel's head—and snapped the angel's neck like a twig.

Chapter 24
DEUS EX MACHINA

Staring through a haze of pain, Jonathan watched as Gabriel's limp body crumpled to the floor. No longer an archangel, just a thin, blind old man who'd loved building clocks.

"Grandfather!" he cried as he felt his heart breaking.

It was finally too much for Grimm. Dealing Crow a stunning blow that sent him flying, the big man launched himself at Belial like an artillery shell. The archdemon just stood and watched him come. Grimm raised Isobel for an almighty strike to Belial's head, but he didn't get the chance. With supernatural speed, the archdemon stepped aside and raked festering fingernails across Grimm's back. The big man screamed as if he'd been dipped in acid, then dropped to his knees.

Belial turned to look at Ignatius, a guttural, liquid laugh bubbling up from inside him like marsh gas through stinking mud. The reek of rotten meat that flowed from him was so strong, it made Ignatius want to gag.

"Now for you!" the archdemon spat, hatred burning in his eyes. And a terrible change began to overtake him. His skin rippled as whatever was hiding beneath decided it was time to reveal itself.

"We need to get out of here!" shouted Kenneth, pushing his daughter protectively behind him and starting the change to his wolf form.

"Not without Jonathan," said Ignatius.

"Hurry," said Elgar. "I don't know what's happening to Belial, but it's not going to be good!"

Ignatius took a step toward Jonathan but was brought up short when, with a sound like tearing cloth, Belial's body grew violently in size, the skin on his face stretching obscenely before splitting like old leather. The seams of his suit gave way, the shredded remnants swaddling a pulsating, malformed torso.

"Dear Lord," said Ignatius, his face deathly pale.

"I didn't know he could do that," said Elgar, hiding behind Ignatius's leg.

Belial's body gave one final heave as two huge, membranous wings erupted from his shoulders, the tatters of his suit and skin dropping to the floor with a sound like a wet towel. The change was complete.

Unable to move, Jonathan stared as Belial reared up to his full height and roared at the ceiling, the black scales that covered his thickly muscled body glinting under the ballroom lights. His horned reptilian head, like a nightmare version of Brass, swung down to glare at Ignatius with an open mouth full of mismatched fangs. Crimson droplets spattered onto the wooden floor, and the creature gave vent to a rumbling, viscous chuckle.

"Hiding one's true form can be tiresome," he hissed. "But occasionally I find that showing it is useful for instilling fear. Who would think that you could fit all this" — he spread his arms wide — "into that?" He indicated the stinking pile of flesh that lay oozing on the floor.

Ignatius stood his ground, desperate not to show the fear that flowed through him. "Given that you're an archdemon," he said, "I'd have expected something a little more . . . impressive."

Belial snarled but didn't rise to the bait. He turned his attention to Elgar. "Well, cat," he sneered. "I see that you survived your exile after all. Do you feel comfortable in *your* skin? Have you learned your place yet?"

Elgar hissed furiously, his fur standing on end. "Go to hell!" he spat.

"Not yet, little demon. Not just yet."

With a gesture from Belial, Elgar slumped to the floor as if he'd been struck. He howled in pain, his claws skittering over the polished wood as his limbs flailed helplessly.

"*Stop it!*" screamed Cay. "You're killing him, you monster!"

Elgar snorted his defiance. "Is that all you've got?" he grunted. But the pain was too much; the cat fell unconscious, his breath ragged and shallow.

"Now what?" Ignatius asked Belial as Grimm clambered unsteadily to his feet.

"Now I take my time killing you all." The archdemon inhaled and closed his eyes, savoring the moment. "Killing you all . . . slowly."

"You talk too much," said Ignatius, his teeth clenching his pipe.

The archdemon roared and with lightning speed grabbed the front of Ignatius's jacket and lifted him off his feet. "I think," Belial growled at the vicar, "I'll begin with you!"

Jonathan watched in frozen horror as Ignatius struggled to get free while Grimm threw himself at the huge creature, wielding Isobel with all his strength.

Leaving Cay in the doorway, the wolf launched himself into the fray. Within seconds both he and Grimm were doing their best to stop Belial from killing Ignatius while, unable to move, Jonathan could only scream silently as he watched his friends fight for their lives. He wanted to join them, to unleash the power that he knew lay somewhere inside him, but try as he might he couldn't find it. The block that Belial had placed inside his mind was too strong. And without help, Jonathan knew, it could only be a matter of time before Belial tore his friends to pieces.

Only a matter of time.

For suddenly Jonathan heard a gentle chiming. He didn't recognize it, but it seemed to be coming from his watch. Before his eyes, everything slowed to a crawl and then to a complete stop. The lethal dance with Belial froze midcombat, silence fell upon the ballroom, and the smell of apples and beeswax reached Jonathan's nose. Then, mercifully, he was somewhere else. And he could move again.

He found himself standing on a wide marble platform, hanging in space. Behind him two impossibly tall gates made of glass and gold reached up into the stars. The gates were so high that he couldn't see where they ended, or even if they ended.

Without warning a runaway train full of memories slammed into his mind—images of a terrible battle, of a shining city, of the joy of creation, of falling and of burning. Feeling himself being buried beneath their weight, Jonathan began to panic, clawing at the images as they swirled around him; then, just as it became too much, a pair of familiar hands reached out and grasped his, steadying him until the rush of memories flowed around—but not over—him.

"Hello, grandson," said Gabriel, his face free from injury, his eyes impossibly blue.

"Gabriel?" gasped Jonathan. "But you're dead." His heart ached in his chest as he pictured his grandfather falling to the floor.

"Yes." The angel nodded. "It was the only way to save you all. He doesn't know it yet, but in killing me Belial has doomed himself. It is my gift to you."

"But Belial has done something to me," cried Jonathan. "I couldn't use my power even if I wanted to!"

"Oh, grandson," said Gabriel, smiling at Jonathan with extraordinary warmth. "There is no point getting old if you don't get crafty. Look around you—where do you think you are?"

"I don't know."

"You are standing in a memory of Heaven. My memory of Heaven, back when I was first created. Behind you are the gates, and if you open them, you will see such wonders."

"But the gates are locked."

Gabriel nodded. "But I have given you knowledge. All of my knowledge. Everything I was I give to you. I once thought I would give it to my son, but ever since the day you were born I knew it had to be you. You will be a bastion against the dark — a guardian against the chaos outside of creation."

"But how can I have your memories?" asked Jonathan, bemused.

Gabriel just smiled at him. "If you have my memories, you already know the answer. Look inside yourself. Believe it, know it. See what I have made for you."

Jonathan did as his grandfather asked and realized that the truth had been literally within arm's reach all along. He looked at the watch Gabriel had given him and understood what a gift it had truly been.

"Deus ex machina," he said.

"And you know what it means now, don't you?"

Jonathan nodded. "God from a machine. It's not just a way to control Brass, is it?"

Gabriel shook his head and grinned mischievously.

"It's the back-door key to Heaven too," Jonathan continued, his voice filled with awe.

Gabriel nodded.

"And more than that," said Jonathan, "it was your way of making sure that all your knowledge wasn't lost if you died. Whoever wore this watch at the moment of your death would get it all."

"Deus ex machina," said Gabriel, his face happy beyond measure. "There are so many ways you can find God in a machine."

Jonathan stared at the watch. He could feel it ticking against his wrist. It was warm and reassuring, just like the voice of his wings. His eyes went wide.

"I can hear my wings!" he said. "They're not shouting; they're not angry."

"That's because you have my memories. It will take a long time to master all that power, but I will be there walking beside you while you learn."

Jonathan nodded, tears running down his cheeks as he understood that he would never speak face to face with his grandfather again.

"Now, grandson," said Gabriel, "let me show you what it's like to fly — what it's like to slip the surly bonds of earth and touch the face of God!"

A blow from Belial caught Grimm on the shoulder and knocked him across the floor. Moments later a vicious kick sent Kenneth, in his wolf form, flying through the air to land by the double doors. Free from distraction, Belial bent to devour Ignatius. The vicar of Hobbes End, pipe still gripped between his teeth, closed his eyes and prayed that he had the strength to die well.

"BELIAL!" Cay screamed at the top of her lungs. "LOOK BEHIND YOU!"

The archdemon paused, chuckling to himself. "You really don't expect me to fall for that one, do you, little girl?" he asked.

Ignatius opened his eyes and peered past Belial. His utter astonishment at what he saw almost made him drop his pipe. "No, really," he said to the archdemon. "Look behind you."

The grin on Ignatius's face irritated Belial, and with a snort the archdemon turned round.

Staring back at him with cobalt blue eyes stood Jonathan. His body was covered in black armor, the overlapping plates wrought with exquisite craftsmanship. His neck was patterned with red scales, and two small horns grew from his temples. On his wrist was a small, battered watch with a worn leather strap.

"Jonathan?" said Ignatius.

Jonathan smiled at him and walked forward, the plates of his armor sliding and folding as he moved. It was as though he was encased in molten black glass.

"This ends," he said to Belial, his voice filled with

power and controlled fury. "There'll be no more death here."

The archdemon stood completely still, a wildly grinning Ignatius still dangling from his claws.

"Let him go," ordered Jonathan. *"Now!"*

A look of stunned incomprehension plastered across his monstrous face, Belial opened his claws and let Ignatius fall to the floor. Amazed to still be alive, the vicar of Hobbes End ran to the door, sweeping up Elgar's limp body in his arms as he went.

"What are you?" Belial demanded.

"I've been asking myself that a lot lately," said Jonathan. "Now I know. Let me show you what fear looks like, monster." And he spread his arms wide. There was no pain, no anger — just the song of quantum mathematics surging through his body. As he stood, head bowed, two mighty wings appeared in the air behind him, stretching from his upper back right to the ceiling of the ballroom with myriad ribbons of serrated purple light, each one curling joyfully around its neighbor. Cay clapped her hands together and shouted in pure delight — it was both beautiful and terrible, beyond her wildest imagination.

"How?" roared Belial.

Jonathan held up his left arm. "The real Gabriel's clock," he said, glancing at Ignatius and smiling. "It's not just Heaven's back-door key; it's a means to keep my grandfather's legacy alive. Deus ex machina, Belial. *You wanted it? Well, here it is!*" He thrust his arm forward so the archdemon could see the old wristwatch. *"Do you want to try to take it?"*

"Think of what you're giving up, little general," hissed Belial. "You could stand at my side and rule all of creation."

"DON'T YOU DARE, YOU BUTCHER!" bellowed Jonathan, the air around him rippling with the force of his anger.

Belial backed away, finally realizing what he was up against.

Shifting his attention from the archdemon, Jonathan kneeled by his grandfather's body. With infinite care he gently wrapped it from head to toe in his wing ribbons, and covered by a shining purple shroud, Gabriel's body dissolved into that from which he'd been made: light. Through the windows of Jonathan's wings, the old angel finally returned to the heart of creation.

Jonathan stood and turned to face Belial. "You need to leave now," he called across to his friends. "I want you all to be safe."

"What are you going to—?"

Jonathan didn't give Belial time to finish the question. He knew what he was going to do, and with Gabriel's memories guiding him he finally knew how.

"We are going to slip the surly bonds of earth, monster," he interrupted, sending all his wing ribbons flying toward the archdemon. They whipped around and about him, pinning his wings and arms to his body, squeezing with incredible strength.

Roaring his defiance, Belial lunged at Jonathan, snapping at him with a crazed sawmill of razor-sharp teeth. Jonathan staggered back, narrowly avoiding decapitation. With clenched fists he gave Belial a double-handed blow that drove the archdemon to his knees.

"I SAID, RUN!" Jonathan shouted back over his shoulder.

"Everybody out!" Ignatius bellowed.

At that very moment a groggy Elgar finally came to.

"Hey, Belial!" he yelled as the vicar carried him away. "I hope Jonathan pulls your flippin' wings off!" Then the cat was gone, leaving a trail of obscenities in his wake.

"Are you ready?" Jonathan asked the archdemon.

"For what?" Belial growled.

"This," Jonathan replied. Without hesitation he shot skyward, pulling Belial along with him as he smashed through the ceiling and up into the night . . .

Chapter 25
HIGH FLIGHT

As she ran to the front door, her wolf father at her side, Cay noticed that someone was missing.

"Where's Grimm?" she shouted.

Ignatius cast a worried look over his shoulder. There was no sign of his old friend in the ballroom doorway. "I'll go back and get him when I've got you all outside," he said. "Now come on, we haven't much time!"

They'd just reached the front door when behind them an enormous crash shook the building.

"Everyone get in the car," said Ignatius. "I don't know what Jonathan's going to do, but I think we need to be away from here!"

Grimm stared at the hole in the ceiling made by Jonathan and the thrashing Belial.

"That's going to take some fixing," he said, walking across the parquet floor toward Crow. Having recovered from Grimm's earlier blow, the demon was hammering at a side door with his remaining arm, oblivious to his surroundings as he tried desperately to escape.

Standing behind Crow, Grimm swung Isobel up and over his right shoulder.

"Evening," he said.

Crow spun round, a look of horror on his featureless face.

"I've come to pick up a hat," said Grimm, grinning wickedly as he swung Isobel with all his considerable might. And it was with great satisfaction that Grimm took Crow's head clean off his shoulders.

Ignatius sprinted down the main hallway, a wave of relief flooding through him as Grimm appeared in the ballroom doorway. He had a spare bowler hat under one arm and Isobel under the other.

"Isobel two, demons nil!" said Grimm, grinning from ear to ear.

Ignatius grinned back but knew they had to get clear of the house. *"Car! Now!"* he shouted.

With all the speed they could muster they tore along

the hall, down the steps, and into the waiting Daimler. Jumping into the driver's seat, Grimm pulled the ignition key from his shirt pocket and started the engine.

"Present for you," he said to Cay, tossing her Crow's bowler hat. "Hang on tight!"

"But what about Jonathan?" she cried.

"It's not him you need to worry about," hooted Elgar. "It's the archdemon he's about to tear apart. Floor it, Grimm!"

Revving the engine until it screamed, Grimm spun the old car in a tight loop across the front lawn, flattening several box hedges. Within seconds they were flying down the drive and away from the mansion. It wasn't until the main gates loomed large in the car's headlights that Cay realized they had no way of opening them.

"How are we going to get out?" she shouted over the roar of the engine.

"The fun way!" barked Grimm, his face alight with excitement.

"I take it we're not going to stop, then?" said Ignatius, bracing his feet against the dashboard.

Grimm shook his head and floored the accelerator.

"Hang on, Dad!" Cay said to her father. He hadn't had time to change back to human form, and he looked at her with huge yellow eyes and whined in alarm as he tried to jam himself behind Ignatius's seat.

"You know, Cay," Grimm called over his shoulder, "I've always wanted to do this. Brace yourselves!"

With a terrific bang the car slammed into the iron gates, smashing them open before slewing its way onto the road. One headlight and a considerable portion of the body was destroyed in the process, but the engine kept going. Accompanied by much whooping from Grimm, the old Daimler shot down the country lane, leaving bits of twisted metal in its wake.

High above the mansion, Jonathan used every ounce of his strength to drag the howling Belial up into the night. The urge to rip the archdemon limb from limb was still there, but Jonathan refused to give in to it. He knew what punishment he was going to inflict upon Belial — and it didn't involve a quick death.

The archdemon struggled frantically, clawing and biting as he tried to free himself from the grip of Jonathan's wings. Time and time again he almost got loose, but Jonathan refused to let him go, even though Jonathan's glass armor began to shatter under the appalling onslaught, Belial's claws and teeth leaving him bleeding and battered. He ignored the pain.

Increasing his speed, Jonathan powered upward, away from the earth. The air filled with the acrid reek of ozone as lightning arced around the battling pair. With an ear-splitting boom, angel and archdemon shot through the sound barrier. The wind grew colder and the stars brighter as Jonathan and his struggling prisoner hurtled ever upward until, with shocking abruptness, Jonathan stopped.

With the knowledge of what he was about to do burning blue in his eyes, Jonathan spoke to Belial one last time as they hung there, high above the curve of the moon-bright earth.

"Why did you cause so much pain?" he demanded. "*Why?*"

Belial spat black blood and grinned. "It's in my nature, little general."

Jonathan gritted his teeth. "So be it," he said. "I'm sending you home, monster. Right onto Lucifer's doorstep. Let's see what he decides to do with you!" As a look of shock crossed Belial's face, Jonathan plunged downward, driving the shrieking archdemon before him.

The stars blurred past, and the very air screamed. Jonathan was dimly aware of Belial struggling in his grip again, but he ignored the distraction. All his focus, all Gabriel's knowledge, everything he'd become, was geared to a single task. The memories of the greatest engineer in the universe guided Jonathan in calling forth the formulas needed to punch a new hole in reality. As the mansion loomed large beneath him once more, Jonathan trusted that he'd gotten the timing right.

"This is probably going to hurt!" he said to himself.

"Stop here, Grimm!" shouted Ignatius.

Grimm brought the car to a halt and Ignatius got out, staring over the fields to where the lights of Belial's mansion could still be seen.

"What are we looking at?" asked Elgar, jumping onto the Daimler's roof.

"That," said Ignatius, pointing to a bright purple star streaking earthward at incredible speed. A moment later it struck home, and in the blink of an eye the mansion was vaporized. The force of the blast was extraordinary, chunks of wood and masonry flying in all directions as a wall of air and noise swept over the car.

In seconds it was all over, and silence descended.

"Jonathan?" asked Cay.

"I don't know," said Ignatius. "But we're going to find out."

The car made its way back, carefully skirting lumps of debris in the road. They managed to get halfway up the drive before progress became impossible. In front of them, illuminated by the car headlights, a huge, rubble-strewn crater lay where the mansion had been.

Dust hung thick in the air, and everyone just sat quietly, shocked at the scale of the devastation. Then, as if in answer to their prayers, a figure stumbled out of the gloom. He had no horns growing from his temples, no scales on his neck, no mighty wings; it was just a young boy in torn and filthy clothes.

Ignatius launched himself from the car and ran up to Jonathan, stopping short when he saw the extent of his injuries. Jonathan smiled through cracked lips, one eye swollen completely shut and an awful gash on his forehead bleeding profusely.

"Would you mind giving me a lift home?" he croaked. "I don't think I'm up to flying."

"I think," said Ignatius, a huge lump in his throat, "that we can oblige."

Chapter 26

Memories

After all the excitement the journey home was mercifully peaceful in comparison. On the back seat of the Daimler sat Jonathan, wrapped in a blanket and staring out the window with his one good eye, his arm curled protectively around Elgar. Next to him, a sleeping Cay sat cradled in her father's lap, dreaming of a bright blustery day and a new kite. Kenneth Forrester, finally back in human form and content that his wife wasn't going to kill him when he got home, stroked his daughter's hair and watched her sleep peacefully.

"I didn't kill Belial, you know," said Jonathan.

Ignatius turned to look at him but didn't say anything.

"I handed him over to Lucifer," Jonathan continued. "I thought he could come up with a better punishment than we could. Lucifer must have been really angry when Belial smashed through the roof of his tower!"

"The solution does have an elegant symmetry to it," said Ignatius, astonished at the power required to do such a thing.

Jonathan gave him a sad smile, shut his eyes, and instantly fell asleep.

"He'll be all right," said Grimm, seeing the expression on Ignatius's face. "He's a mystery, but the boy's certainly got guts."

"That he has," said Ignatius. "Talking of guts, how are yours after that swipe Belial gave you?"

"It only hurts when I laugh." Grimm winced.

"I'd better not crack any jokes, then," said Ignatius with a grin.

Unable to resist the temptation, Elgar sang out, "There was a young man from Venus, who had an unusual—"

"*No, cat!*" barked Ignatius and Grimm simultaneously.

No one got up too early the following morning. Grimm lay snoring on the sofa in the lounge, a mug of cold tea balanced on his chest. Jonathan was tucked up in bed with Elgar across his feet, and Cay slept between her parents, her mother refusing to let her out of her sight.

In his study, Ignatius was fast asleep in a chair by the fireplace. In his hand was the silver-framed photograph of Angela and David that normally sat on his desk. For the first time in three years he dreamed of his wife and son without feeling the awful pain of their loss. He smiled to himself and settled deeper into the chair.

"They're sort of fuzzy," said Jonathan, sitting at the kitchen table. "I have all of these memories whizzing around in my head. Some are mine and some are Gabriel's. It's weird seeing Mom and Dad through someone else's eyes."

"Yes, it must be," said Ignatius.

"I can see Mom leaving me in Gabriel's cottage, and I can see how sad she was. She didn't abandon me like I thought."

"No," said Ignatius, "she didn't abandon you. She did the only thing she could think of to keep you safe. She brought you home."

Jonathan nodded. "Home," he said. "It's a nice word. It means not having to look over your shoulder; it means not having to run anymore. Hopefully, once Mom hears the news that Belial is gone, she'll know it's safe to come back to Hobbes End."

"Home also means kippers in the fridge and somewhere warm to have a snooze," said Elgar. "Added to which it's a good job you didn't lose your watch. We'd all be dead, and Belial would still be stomping around with his big stinky feet. Are you sure you didn't pull off his wings like I asked you to?"

Jonathan smiled and gently stroked Elgar's fur. "You're a very bad cat," he said.

"That, sir, I take as a compliment."

"You were amazing, Johnny," said Cay. "Can you still fly and stuff?"

"Not yet," said Jonathan. "When I fought Belial I could feel Gabriel's soul guiding me, but he's gone now. His memories are all in my head, though. I just need time to understand them, find out what I can do."

"It was still amazing," said Ignatius. "And you saved all our lives. Bless you, my boy, and bless Gabriel, too, wherever he is."

"Grandfather did what he promised," said Jonathan. "This watch can open a gate to Heaven, but getting it to work is incredibly complicated. The knowledge is all in my head, but knowing and understanding are not the same thing. I have to figure it out, Ignatius. I can't save Dad if I don't." Jonathan bit back tears as he thought about his father still lying injured and alone.

Ignatius patted Jonathan's arm reassuringly. "You'll

figure it out, lad, and soon. Don't struggle to find the answer — just let Hobbes End help you. And when your mom arrives she'll be there for you too. You need to rest for a day and gather your strength. You fought an arch-demon and won, remember, and you've got the scars to prove it."

"Yeah," said Jonathan, looking at the reflection of his battered face in the window. "It's funny knowing that I don't actually look like this. I've got these little horns and some scales like Mom, but now I can choose how I appear. The knowledge of how to mask myself is there in Gabriel's memories."

"And what do you choose to look like?" asked Ignatius.

"Right now I choose to look like me," said Jonathan. "I don't want to scare the postman."

Ignatius grinned.

"Anyway, while I figure out how to find Dad, I'd like to stay here, try to keep out of trouble . . . if that's okay with you?"

Ignatius nodded. "Of course it's okay, Jonathan. You're family. And talking of family, Elgar, we'll try to find out where your parents and brother are too. It's the least we can do after the bravery you've shown."

"Cheers very much," said Elgar.

"You know, I'm really going to miss Gabriel," said

Ignatius. "When I go see Angela and David later today, I think I'll say a prayer for Gabriel, too."

"Thank you," said Jonathan. "Would you mind if I went with you?"

"Of course not," smiled Ignatius.

Suddenly an almighty roar erupted from the direction of the village green.

"What's happening?" asked Jonathan.

"Celebratory cricket match," said Ignatius. "It was Grimm's idea. He even asked Brass if she wanted to be wicketkeeper. Grimm was a bit grumpy when I told him he couldn't use Isobel, though. The number of cricket balls he's lost using that bat is quite extraordinary. He hits them so phenomenally hard. Go on, lad, have some fun — you've earned it."

"You're right, it does sound like fun," said Jonathan. "Come on, Cay, Elgar. Let's go join in."

"Can I be umpire?" asked the cat.

"Better ask Grimm," said Cay. "Oh, by the way, what's this I hear about you actually being a demon?"

"What was it Ignatius said?" said Elgar, doing his best-ever vicar impression. "'Whoever heard of a talking cat?'"

"'Honestly!'" said Jonathan.

Cay laughed. "You're impossible!"

"Yeah," said Elgar. "But you love me for it. Race you!"

With a thundering of feet and paws, Jonathan, Cay, and the cat ran out of the vicarage just in time to see Grimm hit a well-bowled cricket ball with astonishing power. It arced out over the forest and disappeared from sight.

"There goes another one!" Elgar said, laughing. Together the three friends sprinted off down the drive.

EPILOGUE

At the edge of the forest a tall woman in a long black dress stood gazing at the entrance to Hobbes End. She was holding a cricket ball that had just plummeted from the sky, narrowly missing her head.

With a wry smile she strode forward until lost from view beneath the trees.

The archangel Sammael Morningstar was coming home . . .

Author's Note

On pages 222, 267, and 271, Gabriel paraphrases from a poem. The poem is called "High Flight" and was written by Pilot Officer John Gillespie Magee Jr. on August 18, 1941. At the time, he was flying with the Royal Canadian Air Force during World War Two.

He was inspired to write the poem after flying his Spitfire at 33,000 feet. After landing he finished the poem and sent it to his parents on the back of a letter. Three months later, in December 1941, he was killed in a tragic midair collision and was buried in Scopwick cemetery, Lincolnshire, England. He was nineteen years old.

Hobbes End is partly inspired by the beautiful Norfolk village of Heydon, one of the few remaining privately owned villages in England. It remains wonderfully unspoiled, with the most recent building being the Queen Victoria commemorative well built in 1887. The only thing missing is a large pond.

Corvidae is the Latin name for a family of birds containing, among others, rooks, crows, and ravens. Their respective collective nouns are a parliament, a murder, and an unkindness.

Hilton Pashley
Norwich, November 2013